WHERE DID SHE GO?
DI SALLY PARKER
BOOK NINE

M A COMLEY

ACKNOWLEDGMENTS

Special thanks as always go to @studioenp for their superb cover design expertise.

My heartfelt thanks go to my wonderful editor Emmy and my proofreader Joseph for spotting all the lingering nits.

Thank you also to my amazing ARC Group who help to keep me sane during this process.

To Mary, gone, but never forgotten. I hope you found the peace you were searching for my dear friend. I miss you each and every day.

To my rock, my Mum for the good days and the bad that we're having to deal with at the moment. Dementia sucks. But what doesn't kill us makes us stronger. Love you always.

ALSO BY M A COMLEY

Blind Justice (Novella)

Cruel Justice (Book #1)

Mortal Justice (Novella)

Impeding Justice (Book #2)

Final Justice (Book #3)

Foul Justice (Book #4)

Guaranteed Justice (Book #5)

Ultimate Justice (Book #6)

Virtual Justice (Book #7)

Hostile Justice (Book #8)

Tortured Justice (Book #9)

Rough Justice (Book #10)

Dubious Justice (Book #11)

Calculated Justice (Book #12)

Twisted Justice (Book #13)

Justice at Christmas (Short Story)

Prime Justice (Book #14)

Heroic Justice (Book #15)

Shameful Justice (Book #16)

Immoral Justice (Book #17)

Toxic Justice (Book #18)

Overdue Justice (Book #19)

Unfair Justice (a 10,000 word short story)

Irrational Justice (a 10,000 word short story)

Seeking Justice (a 15,000 word novella)

Caring For Justice (a 24,000 word novella)

Savage Justice (a 17,000 word novella)

Justice at Christmas #2 (a 15,000 word novella)

Gone in Seconds (Justice Again series #1)

Ultimate Dilemma (Justice Again series #2)

Shot of Silence (Justice Again series #3)

Taste of Fury (Justice Again series #4)

Crying Shame (Justice Again series #5)

To Die For (DI Sam Cobbs #1)

To Silence Them (DI Sam Cobbs #2)

To Make Them Pay (DI Sam Cobbs #3)

To Prove Fatal (DI Sam Cobbs #4)

To Condemn Them (DI Sam Cobbs #5)

To Punish Them (DI Sam Cobbs #6)

To Entice Them (DI Sam Cobbs #7)

To Control Them (DI Sam Cobbs #8)

To Endanger Lives (DI Sam Cobbs #9)

To Hold Responsible (DI Sam Cobbs #10)

Forever Watching You (DI Miranda Carr thriller)

Wrong Place (DI Sally Parker thriller #1)

No Hiding Place (DI Sally Parker thriller #2)

Cold Case (DI Sally Parker thriller#3)

Deadly Encounter (DI Sally Parker thriller #4)

Lost Innocence (DI Sally Parker thriller #5)

Goodbye My Precious Child (DI Sally Parker #6)

The Missing Wife (DI Sally Parker #7)

Truth or Dare (DI Sally Parker #8)

Where Did She Go? (DI Sally Parker #9)

Web of Deceit (DI Sally Parker Novella with Tara Lyons)

The Missing Children (DI Kayli Bright #1)

Killer On The Run (DI Kayli Bright #2)

Hidden Agenda (DI Kayli Bright #3)

Murderous Betrayal (Kayli Bright #4)

Dying Breath (Kayli Bright #5)

Taken (DI Kayli Bright #6)

The Hostage Takers (DI Kayli Bright Novella)

No Right to Kill (DI Sara Ramsey #1)

Killer Blow (DI Sara Ramsey #2)

The Dead Can't Speak (DI Sara Ramsey #3)

Deluded (DI Sara Ramsey #4)

The Murder Pact (DI Sara Ramsey #5)

Twisted Revenge (DI Sara Ramsey #6)

The Lies She Told (DI Sara Ramsey #7)

For The Love Of… (DI Sara Ramsey #8)

Run for Your Life (DI Sara Ramsey #9)

Cold Mercy (DI Sara Ramsey #10)

Sign of Evil (DI Sara Ramsey #11)

Indefensible (DI Sara Ramsey #12)

Locked Away (DI Sara Ramsey #13)

I Can See You (DI Sara Ramsey #14)

The Kill List (DI Sara Ramsey #15)

Crossing The Line (DI Sara Ramsey #16)

Time to Kill (DI Sara Ramsey #17)

Deadly Passion (DI Sara Ramsey #18)

Son of the Dead (DI Sara Ramsey #19)

Evil Intent (DI Sara Ramsey #20)

I Know The Truth (A Psychological thriller)

She's Gone (A psychological thriller)

Shattered Lives (A psychological thriller)

Evil In Disguise – a novel based on True events

Deadly Act (Hero series novella)

Torn Apart (Hero series #1)

End Result (Hero series #2)

In Plain Sight (Hero Series #3)

Double Jeopardy (Hero Series #4)

Criminal Actions (Hero Series #5)

Regrets Mean Nothing (Hero series #6)

Prowlers (Di Hero Series #7)

Sole Intention (Intention series #1)

Grave Intention (Intention series #2)

Devious Intention (Intention #3)

Cozy mysteries

Murder at the Wedding

Murder at the Hotel

Murder by the Sea

Death on the Coast

Death By Association

Merry Widow (A Lorne Simpkins short story)

It's A Dog's Life (A Lorne Simpkins short story)

A Time To Heal (A Sweet Romance)

A Time For Change (A Sweet Romance)

High Spirits

The Temptation series (Romantic Suspense/New Adult Novellas)

Past Temptation

Lost Temptation

Clever Deception (co-written by Linda S Prather)

Tragic Deception (co-written by Linda S Prather)

Sinful Deception (co-written by Linda S Prather)

PROLOGUE

"Close your eyes," Ben told her for the umpteenth time.

"But where are we going? You know how much I detest surprises."

"Well, I can't understand why, and hey, you'd better get used to it, life is full of surprises when I'm involved."

The door creaked open. Ben had always been intrigued by old buildings, and he'd had his eye on this place for a while. Tonight, though, he'd summoned up enough courage to take the plunge and come here, with one intention in mind. He and Isabel had been seeing each other for over a month now, and he felt the time was right to take their relationship to the next level. Every conquest, at least in his book, had to be different from the last, hence the reason he'd brought Isabel here, to this derelict property that had caught his interest.

He'd placed a blindfold over Isabel's eyes and led the way carefully up the cracked concrete path, through the overgrown wilderness that, he presumed, had once consisted of a pretty cottage garden.

Isabel tilted her head and asked, "What's that noise, and why does it smell funny all of a sudden?"

"Where's your sense of adventure? Trust me. I would never put you in danger."

"Trust you? Are you kidding me? At the end of the day, Ben, we barely know each other."

His heart sank, and he paused. *Am I doing the right thing? She's been giving me the signals lately that she wanted to take things further, or had she? Maybe I'm guilty of misreading what's been emanating from her. It wouldn't be the first time. Damn!*

His excitement waned, and he removed the blindfold. It took a while for Isabel's eyes to get accustomed to her surroundings, and she visibly shuddered and clutched her arms in a hug.

"What the...? Where are we? Why have you brought me here? What are you up to, Ben?" She backed up a few paces and turned her ankle on some of the crumbled pieces of wall littering the floor behind her.

Ben held up his hands. "I'm sorry, my bad. It was my intention to surprise you."

Eyebrows raised, Isabel took in her surroundings and shook her head. "I have to tell you, you've definitely succeeded on that score. Why bring me here, to this dump?"

He watched her demeanour change before his eyes. Her once fun-loving spirit, that he'd grown to admire since they had started dating, had been replaced by a shadow of uncertainty. Forgetting about her injured ankle, she continued to back up towards the door.

Deflated, he shrugged. "Sorry, I got this so wrong. I thought you would be up for this."

"What's *this*? Why would I want to get dressed up to go on a date with you, only to end up in a dump like this? None of this is making any sense to me, and I'm standing here wondering if I've done the right thing at all, agreeing to go out with you. I'm out of here."

"You can't go. I'm not ready to leave yet. I've been dying to explore this place since, oh, I don't know when. It's been drawing me in for years."

"Fine. Do your zapper thing, and I'll sit in the car while you wade through this shithole. I want no part of it, you hear me?"

His shoulders slumped, and he stood anchored to the spot, surrounded by the remnants of the decaying building as she stomped back to the car. He had no intention of going after her, not now that he'd summoned up the courage to come here tonight, to break into the place, not that it had taken much effort to do it.

He straightened his back, determined to get on with his adventure and proceeded into the next room. He found the same in there, only on a grander scale as the ceiling was hanging down in places. A fleeting doubt drifted through his mind. Should he cut his losses and go back to the car or should he plough on? His surroundings proved to be too enticing to ignore, and he wandered into the hallway, his eye drawn to the staircase that was still remarkably intact. Not surprising, considering they appeared to be made of oak, unlike today's new-builds where MDF ruled.

The first tread creaked as much as the door had when he'd entered the property and, undeterred, he ascended the stairs, his gaze shifting all around him under the glare of the torch on his phone. He aimed the light at the ceiling; it was definitely dodgy in parts, something he would need to be aware of as he continued on his journey.

There were four doors on that level. He predicted it was relatively sound, given the state of the downstairs. At least, that was his initial thought, from his position at the top of the stairs. He pushed open the first door. It was a tiny bedroom. The ceiling was in a bad way. He looked through the gap above his head. The roof had gaping holes in it, and it was obvious the weather had caused much of the damage surrounding him. He backed out of the room and continued along the small hallway to the next door. There was a large bed in one corner, and the rest of the room was chock-full of boxes of varying sizes. He was wise enough not to enter, he could see the carpet had shifted and had dipped into the room below.

Ben retreated and opened the next door. With the floor showing less signs it was about to cave in beneath him, he ventured into the room. The window was cockeyed and hanging in its frame by a thread. A gust of wind got up outside, again, making him wonder if he should be up here at all. Instead of retreating, his interest piqued further, and he cautiously inched his way into the room.

A bed was the dominant feature, dressed in an orange, flowery nylon bedspread that probably dated back to the nineteen seventies. There was a slight bulge underneath it. Ben knew it couldn't be the owner of the house who had died over six years ago; he vaguely remembered her funeral being in the local press.

It's probably a load of blankets and bedding shoved under there. Why isn't this place empty? Didn't the family care about the old woman and her possessions?

The floor moved slightly beneath his feet, but he was determined to investigate what was under the bedspread. What was the point of him coming here if he chose to ignore his inquisitive nature? The floor moved more the closer he got to the bed, as if groaning because of the extra weight.

Crash! He didn't have time to adjust his footing as the floor gave way beneath him. He cried out and followed the bed down to the lounge below. Thankfully, landing on the mattress broke his fall.

Jesus, I hadn't expected that to happen. All good fun, nonetheless. You wait until I tell Isabel, she'll be doubled over in hysterics.

The cloud of dust overwhelmed him for minutes rather than seconds. He bided his time and waited for it to settle once more and then shifted off the bed. The floor was now more littered than before with the added remnants from the ceiling above now lying in a heap all around him, but it was the bed that drew his eye. More to the point, the bones poking out from underneath the bedspread. He stepped forward to take a closer look. His heart pounded, beating out an unhealthy rhythm that rattled his soul.

"What the fuck is that?" He inched nearer to inspect the bones further. "Jesus, it can't be!"

His courage growing, he pulled back the bedspread and peeked underneath. Ben gasped and stumbled backwards, ending up on his arse, staring at the limp remains dangling from the bed.

Time stood still for several minutes, his mind whirling with different scenarios, none of which made any sense. It was that which eventually prompted him to leave the house. He ran back to the car. Isabel was talking to a friend on her phone and ended the call as soon as he jumped into the driver's seat beside her.

"Well, it's about bloody time. Take me home."

Shocked, he shook his head and glanced back at the house. "We can't leave yet."

"What the fuck are you talking about? Don't try any funny business with me, Ben, I ain't into shit like that. I ain't doing it in the car, if that's what you're getting at."

"I'm not. I promise."

Frowning, Isabel placed a hand on top of his. "What's wrong with you? You're shaking. What was in there?"

"I can't... I need to call the police."

"What? Why? Tell me, for God's sake, you're scaring the shit out of me."

He reached for her phone. "Can I borrow it? I dropped mine inside when I fell and didn't get the chance to search for it."

"You fell? You're not making any sense. Are you hurt?"

"No, only my pride. I'll explain what happened in a sec, I need to contact the police."

"Here you go. I knew it was a bloody mistake, you bringing me here. I have a sixth sense about these things."

"I wish you had shared that with me before… yes, I want the police… yes, it's an emergency. I've discovered a dead body."

"What?" Isabel shouted.

CHAPTER 1

Sally was settled down after a hard day at the station. She and Simon had decided to share a nice bottle of red from his bulging cellar. She had every intention of finishing off that bottle of wine, too, after the mind-numbing day she'd had.

She closed her eyes and revelled in the fact that she had the finer things in life, thanks to marrying Simon several years ago. His property renovation business was doing far better than either of them had anticipated and had taken an upward swing since their good friend, Tony Warner, had agreed to join her husband.

"I knew it would work out with you two. Lorne and I are both envious that we're not involved in the business, especially Lorne. You know how adept she is in the interior design department."

"I loved her ideas on the last project we worked on. Her colour scheme was impactful and definitely secured us maximum profit on that project. Tony has a great eye for detail as well. We make a great team, bringing different skills to the table. I know I got on great with your dad, but we're talking a different level here entirely. Your father realises that the business is thriving with Tony on board."

"He does. I'll be forever grateful to you for keeping him on, what with his ill health, if only in a minor role."

"Nonsense, his input is just as valuable as Tony's and mine. Without him being on site, ensuring the men cover all the necessary work to put the houses on the market, we'd be lost. It frees Tony and me up to search for yet more challenging projects that will bring us in far more profit next time."

"It's all about the teamwork, and you definitely make a great team. Just like Lorne and I did on that last case we solved together a few years back when she was serving with the Met Police. I'm thrilled to have enticed her out of retirement, she's such a pleasure to work with. Her instincts as a copper are second to none."

"What are you saying? I know that look, there's something going on in that head of yours."

She laughed. "Ha, you think you know me so well; in this case you're wrong. Jack is my partner for as long as he wants the job. I would never ditch him or move him aside to make room for Lorne, no matter how tempted I am. I'd feel a right bitch doing that. It's just great having her on the team with us."

"Yeah, I know you would. Although, it doesn't stop you contemplating a way around the issue, does it?" He chinked his glass against hers and laughed.

"No comment," Sally admitted. She took a satisfying sip from her full-bodied red and then groaned when her phone vibrated on the table beside her. "Damn, I knew it was too good to be true."

"Ignore it. You're entitled to your time off, darling. You've given the Norfolk Constabulary the best years of your life, and now it's time to start enjoying our evenings together."

She knew he was right, but her hand twitched nervously and hovered over the phone all the same. "Sorry, I have to. It wouldn't feel right ignoring it."

He hitched up a shoulder and patted Dex on the head. "Who am I to argue with her? What's the point anyway, eh, boy?"

Dex groaned and placed his head on Simon's lap.

"Stop ganging up on me, you two. It is what it is. Like it or lump it." She answered the phone on the fourth ring. "DI Sally Parker, how can I help?"

"Sorry to disturb you, ma'am, it's Jill from the control centre. A body has been discovered at a house out near Thetford Forest. I wondered if you wouldn't mind attending."

"Isn't there anyone else on duty?"

"There was a pile-up earlier this evening, and a lot of our guys are out there, lending a hand. Lots of fatalities to contend with, apparently."

"Say no more." Sally held her glass up and assessed how much she had drunk. "You're lucky I haven't had a skinful tonight. I had every intention of sharing the evening with my husband and a couple of bottles of red."

"I'm so sorry to interrupt your evening."

"What's done is done. You'd better give me the address, Jill."

"Thank you. It's number eight Warburton Lane. There are only a few cottages down there. This house hasn't been lived in for about six years. It's in a sorry state, ma'am, so I wouldn't bother showing up there in your best clobber."

"Thanks for the warning. I'll go as I am then. I'll be there in twenty minutes. Do me a favour and call my partner, Jack Blackman, ask if he'll attend the scene with me."

"I'll get onto him right away, ma'am. I appreciate you going the extra mile on this one. So sorry to have called you in. If you'll pass on my apologies to your husband…"

"Don't worry, he's used to us having our evenings disrupted."

"Very well, ma'am. I'll leave you to it."

"Thanks, Jill. I'd say it's been a pleasure, but you know, in the circumstances, I won't bother."

They both laughed, and Sally ended the call.

She leaned over and kissed Simon. "I'm sorry, I tried my hardest to get out of it."

"I heard. Go, if you have to. We're not going to fall out about this, Sally, however, I'll add a word of caution and tell you that you need to put your foot down now and again. Running the Cold Case team was supposed to give you more time off. Let me know tomorrow how that's working out for you."

"Ouch, that's harsh, hon. They wouldn't call me if it wasn't important."

"I know. I'm sorry for snapping. You go, maybe Dex will help me polish off the bottle in your absence."

Sally chuckled. "I can imagine the pair of you staggering your way up to bed." She kissed him and then pecked Dex on the nose. "Take care of your dad for me, and no getting up to any funny business when my back is turned, you hear me?"

Dex moaned and licked her face.

"That's good enough for me." She sat up and ran a hand down Simon's face. "I'm genuinely sorry for spoiling our evening together. Hopefully, I won't be out long."

"Hmm… where have I heard that before? We'll see you when we see you. Take care and drive safely."

"It's far lighter at this time of year, so there's no need to worry on that score." She gave her husband a final kiss on the lips and dipped into the hallway. She appraised her appearance in the ornate full-length mirror and decided the jogging pants and sweatshirt she'd thrown on earlier, once she'd got home from work, would suffice for the occasion. Slipping on a pair of trainers completed her ensemble. She picked up her keys from the dish on the console table and headed out of the front door.

JACK WAS ALREADY at the scene. "What the heck are we doing out here at this time of night? If you hadn't requested my attendance, I would have told them to shove their invitation where the sun don't shine."

"Sorry, mate. I was tucked up on the sofa as well, enjoying a glass of wine. What do you know, anything?"

"Not really. I've only been here a couple of minutes. Have you seen the state of this place? It's derelict."

"Yep, I noticed. Let's have a word with whoever is on site to get the lowdown on what we have here."

Jack pointed at the car in front of his that Sally had missed when she'd arrived. "I take it this has something to do with them."

"There's only one way to find out."

With that, a uniformed copper came out of the building.

"And you are?" he asked.

Sally smiled. "DI Sally Parker, called out to attend the scene, and yes, I didn't bother getting changed. What's going on?"

"Ah, sorry. I recognise you now, ma'am. The young couple put the call in. The bloke was inside the house, haven't figured out why yet. He was upstairs, and the floor gave way. He came tumbling down, landed on the bed and discovered there was a dead body on the mattress."

"Shit! How dead? Has the pathologist been informed?"

"Very dead. I'd say the likelihood of the person being deceased for several years is quite high, ma'am. And yes, the pathologist is on her way, she was dealing with another scene."

"The pile-up?"

"Not as far as I know, ma'am."

"It doesn't matter. Rather than get togged up in our protective gear, we'll have a chat with the witnesses first."

"As you wish, ma'am," the young officer said.

Sally and Jack made their way over to the car. The man was comforting the woman in the front seat. He saw them coming and leapt out of the car.

"I didn't do it, I swear I didn't," he blurted out, much to Sally's amusement.

She smiled, doing her absolute best to put him at ease. "First things first, what's your name, sir?"

"Ben Dougal. I know I sound like a blithering idiot, but seeing that… er, skeleton like that, it's kind of freaked me out."

"I'm sure it has. I'm DI Sally Parker, and this is my partner, Jack Blackman. Would it be all right if we spoke in the car?"

"I have to know if you're going to arrest me." Ben ran a trembling hand through his cropped black hair.

"Of course not. Look, we're not in the habit of arresting people just because they've discovered a corpse. That is, unless you have something to hide?"

"No way. Like what? It was a total shock finding those bones in the bed like that. At first, I thought it was the old woman who used to live there but then I remembered reading about her funeral in the local paper and realised it couldn't be her. There I go again, with the verbal diarrhoea. My brain is working overtime, and apparently, so is my tongue."

"Don't worry, it's a natural response for some people. Please, get in the car. Is that your wife?"

"I wish. No, it's my girlfriend. I think I've screwed things up between us, though."

Sally inclined her head and frowned. "How come?"

"I brought her here to... well, you know, take our relationship to the next level. Yeah, I know, there's no need for you to tell me what a plonker I am."

Jack cleared his throat beside Sally. She stamped on his foot when Ben shrugged and opened the car door.

"What did I do?" Jack complained.

"Leave it. Can't you see how upset the poor bloke is?"

"Yeah, only because he's messed up his love life."

"Harsh, Jack, very harsh. Get in the back and make yourself useful. Get your notebook out and keep your wise cracks and sniggers to yourself for the next twenty minutes or so."

"I'm beginning to wonder why I bothered coming out here at all."

Sally smiled, opened the back door and climbed in. "Hi, I'm DI Sally Parker," she introduced herself to the young woman whimpering in the front seat.

"I'm Isabel. Is this going to take long? We did the right thing calling nine-nine-nine. I didn't expect us to still be out here almost an hour later. What took you so long to get here?"

"Issy, that's not very nice," Ben reprimanded her. He cast a glance over his shoulder at Sally.

"No, it's fine. We were actually off duty after already completing a ten-hour shift today. We wouldn't have needed to attend the scene if half the force weren't needed at the major pile-up on the other side of town."

Isabel gasped and cried again before she mumbled an apology that Sally had to strain her ear to catch.

"It's okay. Right, why don't you tell us what happened here tonight?"

"We showed up at the house around an hour and a half ago. I was wrong to bring Isabel here, she had no idea what I was up to."

"At last, you've finally admitted you're in the bloody wrong," Isabel agreed bitterly.

"Anyway, Isabel was livid and came back to the car. I was really intrigued about the place. I've passed it loads of times and always wanted to have a nose around on the inside."

"Any particular reason?" Sally asked.

"I'm interested in architecture and want to get into property developing, when I've built up enough funds, that is."

"Ah, I see. It takes a lot of cash to go down that route."

"She should know, her husband is a property developer," Jack threw in.

Sally smacked her knee against his.

"He is?" Ben asked. He twisted in his seat, his eyes wide with enthusiasm. "How successful is he?"

Sally smiled. "Quite successful. He gave up his job as the local pathologist to follow his dreams."

"Christ, I'm really envious of him. It's been my ambition to get a foothold on the buy-to-let market for years."

"You should take the plunge but you're going to need an excellent team of builders to fulfil your dreams once you've signed the paperwork."

"Yeah, I realise that. My brother is the key there. He's a builder and has a group of mates from all the trades needed to turn a house around within a few months."

"Gee, I hate to break this up, but I'm keen to get home," Isabel said and heaved out an impatient breath.

Sally nodded. "Sorry, Isabel, yes, you're right, we should concentrate on the task in hand, I apologise."

"Yeah, I'm sorry, too, Isabel, this is neither the time nor the place to speak about such issues, not when there's a dead body to consider. When will you know who it is?" Ben asked.

Sally shrugged. "It depends on the decomposition of the remains. We'll know more when the pathologist arrives."

"I'm no expert but" Ben began.

"Jesus, here we bloody go," Isabel groaned.

"What?" Ben queried. "I'm only telling the inspector that I've seen a few cold cases on TV."

"And that makes you a damn expert all of a sudden? You're such a tosser at times," Isabel slung back at him.

"That's uncalled for, Issy."

"It's Isabel, idiot. Only my family are allowed to call me Issy, got that?"

Ben puffed out his cheeks with a long sigh. "Consider me told. Can you stop snapping at me? We've both been through a bad experience, me more than you. I was the one who fell through the ceiling, I might add."

"I didn't realise it was a sodding competition, arsehole."

"That's enough," Sally intervened. "Falling out about this isn't going to get either of you very far, is it?"

"She's right, Iss… abel. Can't we at least try to get along, long enough for us to give the police our statements?"

"I suppose."

"Good. Perhaps you can tell us how you got into the house in the first place?" Sally aimed her question at Ben.

"I came here during the day to have a scout around. Went through the back door and then walked through the house to unlock the front door for when we arrived."

Sally raised an eyebrow. "You had it all figured out then."

"Yeah, it sounds like it, doesn't it?" Isabel mumbled. "I still can't believe you'd bring me here for… at all."

"I'm sorry." Ben flung his hands up in the air. "How many more times do I have to say it?"

"If you said it a hundred times a day for the next thirty years it still wouldn't matter, I don't believe you."

"Whatever," Ben replied. "Anyway, we went inside the house and started walking around the place. I was intrigued, wanted to go upstairs, but little Miss Scaredy Pants here had other ideas. She refused to stay in there, so I told her to come back to the car while I had a nose around myself. I went upstairs, had to pick my way around up there. I knew I was taking a risk and refused to go in some of the rooms, but something caught my attention in the main bedroom. Thinking the floor was more stable in there, I decided to investigate what was under the covers. I crept closer to the bed, and that's when the floor gave way beneath me. The bed went down first, so I had a soft landing, but then…"

"You landed on the remains as well?" Sally finished off his sentence for him.

"Yeah. I kind of froze for a moment or two while the dust settled around me and then legged it. I got back to the car and rang nine-nine-nine right away."

"I wanted to leave, but he told me we had to stick around and face the music together. I did nothing wrong in there. He's to blame for any destruction or tampering with a crime scene, so please don't come down heavily on me, I'm not taking the fall for this."

"Don't worry. I can assure you that neither of you is in trouble," Sally said.

Ben looked at Sally, relieved, and sighed. "How do you think the body got in there?"

Sally shrugged. "It was probably dumped there. I don't suppose you know who the property belongs to now, do you? I mean, you did mention you had an interest in it."

"No, I never found out. I did try. Maybe the old lady died intestate, is that what they call it?"

Sally smiled and nodded. "That's right. We'll do some digging, see what we can find out. Any idea of the exact date of her death? The property owner I'm talking about."

"No, it was either six or seven years ago."

"Can you tell me her name?"

"Don't quote me on this, but either Edna or Edwina or was it Edith? No clue as to her surname, sorry. I suppose it might come to me later, you know, once my head is a bit clearer and not in a jumbled state like it is right now."

"I'll give you my card, if and when you think of anything, you can get in touch." She handed each of them a card.

"I don't need one, I won't have anything to add." Isabel folded her arms and refused to take it.

Ben took his and rolled his eyes as if offering up a silent apology.

Sally smiled, accepting the situation for what it was. "Would it be all right if we took your phone numbers, just in case any questions arise in the near future?"

"Of course." Ben reeled his off, and Jack jotted it in his notebook.

"Why do you need mine?" Isabel asked. "I barely set foot in the damn place, and here you are, badgering me to give you my private information."

"I wouldn't class it as badgering, but if you don't want to give it to us, that's fine. However, what I will need from both of you in the next day or so is a statement of the events."

Isabel turned in her seat and glared at Sally who was expecting the young woman to go on the attack with a barrage of words. But she sensibly backed down and faced the road again, crossing her arms even tighter.

"I'm sorry you had to get involved in this issue, Isabel." Sally felt the need to apologise for some reason to the young woman.

"Yeah, you and me both. Can we go now?"

"Yes, you're free to go. I hope you understand the necessity for us to have a word with you before you left the scene."

"No, not really. Like I said, all of this shit was to do with him, not me." She jerked her thumb at Ben, and he rolled his eyes once more.

"Nonetheless, thanks for your time and cooperation."

Isabel grunted and sank lower into her seat, her arms still folded tightly across her flat chest.

Sally and Jack left the car. Ben joined them outside the vehicle and closed his door.

"What was I thinking, bringing her here?" he whispered across the top of the car.

Sally smiled. "Maybe you should be more selective where you do your courting next time."

"You're not wrong. Hey, there ain't going to be a next time, not with her anyway. I'm sorry she's been such a grouch with you. I've tried dozens of times to apologise, but she's having none of it. I think the more I said sorry the worse her mood got. Sorry you've taken the brunt of it."

"Hey, it's water off a duck's back to me. You just get her home and get some rest yourself. A uniformed officer will be in touch with you soon, regarding a statement."

"Thanks. I hope you find out who that person is quickly. I suspect you're going to have a hell of a job on your hands there."

"Don't worry, we're used to it. Try not to dwell on things too much."

"I won't. Thanks." He got back in his car and started the engine.

Sally and Jack returned to their vehicle and got togged up in readiness for the forensic team to arrive.

"Hey, speak of the devil and she shall appear," Jack muttered out of the corner of his mouth.

"How to win friends and influence people. Let's get a move on and get in there to take a gander for ourselves."

"What? Before Ms Quiver gets a look at the scene?"

"Not necessarily. From what I can remember, she's not the type to hang around. I bet she's ready to go in half the time we are. I want to be there, to gauge her reaction, as and when she first lays eyes on the body."

"Give her a chance. I know she has a lot to live up to, trying to fill Simon's shoes, but we all had to start somewhere, didn't we?"

"I am giving her a chance. That remark was uncalled for. For your information, I'm also happy Simon gave up the job. Admittedly, in the beginning it was a huge shock. But I wasn't about to stand in the way of his dreams and I'm elated to confirm that he has been proven right. He definitely made the correct decision. I'm using his words here, 'he's as happy as a pig in muck'."

"Wow, that happy, eh?" Jack laughed.

She elbowed him and reached out with a hand to achieve the balance required to step into her paper suit. "You're nuts. Actually, I'd go as far to say that you're nuttier than a squirrel's fart."

Jack pulled the suit up to his waist and stared at her open-mouthed, then he doubled over and expelled a full belly laugh. "I've heard it all now. Where the effing hell did you get that one? Because I know damn well that you didn't just make it up yourself."

"What are you saying? That you don't think I'm capable of making up a great one-liner or two?"

"That's exactly what I'm saying."

She snarled at him. "You can go off some folk, you know. Carry on taking the piss out of me and you'll shoot to the top of my hate list."

Jack pretended to chew his fingers. "Stop, you're scaring the crap out of me."

"Am I interrupting something?" Pauline said when she joined them.

"Not worth the bother repeating it. Nice to see you again, Paul, how's it been going the past few weeks?"

"I think I'm slotting in okay. Of course, I'm not up to your husband's standards just yet but I don't think I'm far off."

They all laughed, but it died down as quickly as it emerged.

"Shall we?" Pauline gestured for Sally to dip under the cordon tape ahead of her.

The officer on duty outside the house opened the front door for them. "You're going to need to mind your footing in there, and for now, the upstairs is off limits as it's been deemed unsafe."

"Thanks for the warning. We'll be careful." Sally resisted the urge to shudder in the damp and dark hallway and picked her way through the filthy entrance into the lounge on the right. "Bloody hell," she said and glanced up at the major hole that had been left in the ceiling.

"You took the words out of my mouth," Pauline said. She cautiously moved closer to the bed in the middle of the room and flipped back the bedspread to reveal the decomposed figure.

"Holy crap." Jack gagged.

Sally pushed him towards the edge of the room. "Over there if you're going to do anything."

He gagged again and then pulled in a deep breath and spluttered.

Sally looked at him and shook her head. "Take it outside, Jack."

He retched his way out into the hallway.

"Sorry about that, he can be such a wuss at times."

"Can't all men? My dad is the same when I go over there for dinner and begin a conversation about a recent case I've been involved in."

"Blimey, you discuss your work at the dinner table? That would freak me out as well."

Pauline chortled. "Thinking about it, maybe that's why I don't receive many dinner invitations from my friends."

Sally laughed. "Bless you, you're welcome to join me

and Simon anytime you like, although I would have to draw the line at you being too open with your conversation."

"Why thank you, I'd love to join you and spend time with the infamous Simon Bracknell. Umm... can I ask a cheeky question before we make a start?"

"Of course, shoot!"

"Why did you decide not to change your name when you got married?"

"Simple reason really, I felt it would have been overcomplicated to do it at work."

"And I take it Simon's okay with your decision?"

"Absolutely. I'll change things when I retire, if I ever get the time to retire."

"Ah, yes. What else will you do with all that spare time on your hands, right?"

Sally guffawed. "I dread to think. We'd better get down to business or Jack will be cursing me out there."

"I bet that happens a lot."

"No comment."

"Okay. Let's see what the remains can tell me. At first glance I would say the victim was female." Pauline pointed at the right leg and left forearm. "Two broken bones."

Sally inched closer to study the bones for herself. "Could that have been from the fall?"

"No indication of that, the bones are the same colour. If it had just happened, there would possibly be fragments of bones on the bed and the inside would have been whiter."

"Of course, silly me."

Pauline wagged her finger. "No chastising yourself, it was a simple enough question that deserved an answer. Ah, what do we have here?" She shuffled closer to the bed and raised the victim's left hand a few inches.

"A wedding and an engagement ring. That's great and will

definitely give us something to go on, I hope. Any chance you can slip them off for me?"

Pauline placed her bag on the floor beside her and extracted a plastic evidence bag. She held the wrist of the victim and jerked it slightly. Both rings slid off and into the bag. Pauline then handed it to Sally. "There's a risk these might drop off, so I'm pre-empting it."

It was hard to make out in the dimming light. "I think I can see some kind of inscription in the wedding ring. The light isn't good enough in here for my aging eyesight."

Pauline smiled. "Christ, I've heard it all now. Let's hope it gives you the lead you need to get the investigation underway. I'd rather not move the body again, until after the photos have been taken. The rest of the team should be here soon. I came on ahead, eager to sink my teeth into this one."

"I love your enthusiasm. I can't say it's infectious. All I'm seeing is a mountain of work ahead of me."

"I'm sure. And you're right, I'm super excited to be involved in a cold case. I love a good challenge, it keeps you on your toes, doesn't it?"

"You're not wrong. Okay, here it is, the question you've been dreading since we met outside."

Pauline smiled and nodded.

"How long has the body been here, any idea?" Sally asked.

Pauline's mouth twisted from side to side as she contemplated the question. "Okay, here's the deal. I can give you a ballpark figure but I don't want you quoting me, not at this early stage. You know there's a lot to be considered before I give you a genuine, more realistic timeframe."

"Yadda yadda, I get that. I promise I won't hold you to anything. A rough guess would be?"

With that, the door opened and Jack entered the room.

"Nice of you to rejoin us, Sergeant."

"Sorry about that. You'll be pleased to know I didn't bring anything up."

Sally raised an eyebrow and shook her head. "What do you want me to do, put the flags out?"

"You can be such a hard woman at times, Inspector," Jack grumbled.

"If you two have quite finished," Pauline jumped in. "To answer your question, I believe we're likely looking at between six and eight years, no, correction, let's call it seven instead."

"Blimey, how can you tell?" Jack asked, his gaze flicking between Pauline and Sally as if he was missing something.

"Several things really, and years of experience in the classroom," Pauline shot back at him.

"Like what?" he countered.

"The decaying of the bones. Of course, that differs immensely in the circumstances in which the body is located."

"You mean the bones would look differently if the body had been buried and dug up?"

Pauline smiled and jerked her thumb at him while speaking to Sally. "He's good."

"Yeah, when he wants to be. He's also keen on being slack at coming forward most days, too."

"I dispute that!" Jack's disgruntled reply came.

Pauline laughed. "I can see I'm going to have a lot of fun working alongside you two."

"We'll definitely brighten your day," Sally admitted.

They spent the next half an hour studying the body and their surroundings, although ideas as to how the body had got there in the first place remained thin on the ground. At nine-thirty, Sally made the executive decision to call it a day.

"I'm relieved," Jack said once they reached the cars.

"We'll make a start on the case in the morning, there's little we can do at this time of night, not on a cold case."

"Rightio. See you bright and early then."

"I'll be there. Enjoy what's left of your evening, Jack."

"I doubt it. Donna had a cob on when I left. We were just about to sit down and watch a movie together as a family, for a change."

"Ouch, sorry. Send her my heartfelt apologies."

"I will."

CHAPTER 2

The following day, Sally had a spring in her step. Simon was up, preparing the breakfast in his dressing gown when she walked into the kitchen. Dex ran to greet her with his favourite toy hanging out of his mouth.

"Drop it, boy." She knew there would be more chance of getting snow in July than getting it off him. He circled the area at her feet and playfully growled every time she reached out a hand. "Sod you then," she said good-naturedly.

"He's a card, isn't he? Sit down, breakfast won't be long."

"I hope there's not too much on the menu today."

"How about a bacon and fried egg sandwich? I thought it would help set you up for the day."

"Sounds perfect, not sure I could have coped with a full English."

"I must have had a sixth sense about it this morning. Anyway, I had some mouldy bread I needed to use up."

Sally's mouth dropped open at the thought.

He laughed and pointed at her. "You can be so gullible at times, as if I would do that to my darling wife."

While Simon's back was turned, Sally snuck a sneaky peek at the slice of bread he was slathering in butter.

Satisfied that he was having her on, she pulled out a chair at the kitchen table and held her face up to the rays of the morning sun filtering through the kitchen window. "Have you got much on today?"

He delivered their sandwiches and sat opposite her. "Tony and I are going to drive around a number of areas today, see if we can spot any bargains new to the market."

She squirted some ketchup on one slice of bread and got ready to take a bite of her sandwich. "What about the estate agents? I thought you had contacts at all the major ones in the area."

"We do, but things seem to have dried up. It'll be good to be out there in the thick of things, checking out different areas, observing what kind of regeneration is going on, you know how much that affects the value of properties these days."

"Ah, yes, I'm with you now, something that you guys really need to consider."

"That's right. What will be first on the agenda for you today with regard to your new case?"

"I'll bring the team up to date and then get them delving into who owns the property, if anyone does."

"They must do, surely, otherwise, wouldn't the council have come along and bulldozed it and erected a block of flats in its place by now?"

She swallowed the mouthful of goodness and replied, "I suppose so, never really thought about that." She winked at him. "Thanks for the tip."

"I have my uses."

"How's Dad been getting on lately?"

"He gets better with age. His eye for detail is now second to none, and he's got a great rapport with the workforce. It used to bug me when I checked on a house and it had a shoddy finish because the workmen had fallen out with each other and taken their eye off the ball. We have none of that when they know your father is keeping a constant eye on their progress."

"I'm delighted it's all working out for the best. You and Tony seem to be getting on like a house on fire, too."

"We are. All in all, I'm extremely happy, and the transition to become a full-time property developer has been far less bumpy than either of us imagined."

"You had doubts?"

"Grave ones, but I kept them to myself rather than let them fester and get in the way."

Sally reached across the table, and they linked hands. "You should have told me."

"I hate any form of negativity, you know that. I was determined to make a go of it and I'm more than satisfied with the outcome."

"You can count that as having two successful professions under your belt now."

"I can. I think another ten years of this and we can both consider packing up and retiring to a sunnier climate."

She paused before taking another bite of her sandwich. "You'd move from here? Leave all our family—correction, my family—and friends come to that?"

A devilish glint formed in his eye. "No, I just wanted to see what your reaction would be if I said it."

"You can be so mean at times."

"I know."

Sally's eye caught the time on the clock, high up on the wall. "Damn, I'd better be going. I told Jack I'd be at the station bright and early this morning."

"Breakfast with your husband is one of life's pleasures that should be savoured and not rushed."

"Whatever." She rose from the table, wiped the grease from her mouth, and then leaned in for a kiss.

Simon had already wiped his mouth, anticipating her next move. "Have a good day. Give me a ring if you have the time later."

"I'll see how it goes. Happy prospecting today. Are you taking Dex with you?"

"Definitely, he's excellent company in the car."

Sally ruffled Dex's head and then caught him off guard and kissed him on the nose. Dex groaned and then covered his nose with his paw.

"Daft dog. You two have fun. Think of me, either being stuck in the office all day or out there, breaking some poor family's hearts, sharing the news of their dearly departed loved one."

He shook his head. "I know which would be my choice. Take care, love you."

"I love you, too. See you around the usual time, unless anything unforeseen crops up later. I'll let you know either way."

He smiled, and she left the kitchen. Outside, she looked back at the house, and he was standing at the window, waving and blowing kisses.

Sally smiled. He was a lot happier these days, not that he was ever a grouch in his former role, well, maybe a little. However, it was still a pleasure to see a smile etched on his face most days.

She arrived at the station the same time as her partner.

"Ha, I don't feel so bad being late now," Jack said.

Sally joined him on the path, and they entered Wymondham Police Station together. Pat Sullivan was on duty behind the desk, as usual.

"Morning, ma'am, Jack. How are you both?"

"Fair to middling, thanks, mate," Jack replied.

Sally jabbed a thumb at her partner, standing behind her. "What he said."

"I hear you've got a new case to keep you on your toes."

"Yep, we're about to get the team brought up to date on it now," Sally responded.

"Don't hesitate to give me a shout if you need anything."

Sally punched her number into the security keypad and threw over her shoulder, "Don't worry, we won't."

Sally switched on the lights in the main office, and Jack carried out his morning duty of putting the kettle on. The rest of the team filtered into the room over the next ten minutes. Lorne was the last to arrive, which was strange for her. Sally made a mental note to have a quiet word in her best friend's ear later, make sure everything was all right at home.

"Gather around, peeps. We've got a new case to sink our teeth into. Last night, Jack and I attended a scene. It was in an abandoned house. A young couple found the body after their plans of making out in the house went awry."

"Christ, I'm not surprised," Lorne said.

"Yeah, I have to agree. You should have seen the state the place was in," Sally replied. "Anyway, the woman, after seeing what a wreck it was, refused to entertain what the chap had in mind. Apparently, he's had his eye on the property for a while and was keen to see what was going on inside. He's a budding property developer."

"Seems to be a popular career nowadays." Lorne chuckled.

"So, the woman left the house, and Ben, the chap who found the remains, decided to venture upstairs. Why, I couldn't tell you. I wouldn't have, given the state of the house. Curiosity got the better of him, and he crept into the main bedroom after he spotted a shape under the nylon bedspread, I'm betting the type all our grannies had back in the seventies. As he got closer, the floor gave way beneath him. Luckily, the bed broke his fall on its way into the lounge. It kind of freaked him out when he landed on the remains of a body"

"Shit, I'm not surprised," Jordan Reid said. "You wouldn't see me for bloody dust, I can tell you."

The group laughed.

"Nor me," Jack agreed. "The bloody place was tumbling down. You'd have to be nuts entertaining going there for a snoop around, let alone to have sex with your new bird."

"Gives me the shivers just thinking about it," Joanna Tryst said.

"Maybe he had a bet on with one of his mates," Jordan offered. "Who can bed a bird in the weirdest place."

"Wouldn't surprise me," Jack said.

"If we can get back to it, guys? Thank you. Whatever the reasons behind the couple's visit, it happened, and it turned out to be a nightmare situation for both of them. He's to be admired because he left the house and dialled nine-nine-nine, even though he might find himself in trouble for breaking and entering an empty property. Our first priority is to find the owner of the property. According to Ben, he believes the woman died intestate, but I'd much prefer to work with the facts than just hearsay. He also said the old lady who used to reside there was called Edna, Edwina or Edith. Joanna, will you do the necessary digging on that one for me? The address is eight Warburton Lane, Feltwell."

"Of course I will, boss."

"I don't suppose anyone knows that address, do they?"

The other members of the team who had grown up in the area all shook their heads.

"I suppose we could try and get the lowdown from the nearest neighbours," Jack suggested.

"There weren't too many in the area, but there were a few dotted around. Yes, we could start with them. Jordan and Stuart, that can be your task for the day."

"What about the rest of us?" Jack asked. He glanced across the room at Lorne.

"I'd prefer it if we could do the digging needed around here. The pathologist gave us an indication that the body had been dead between six and seven years. Ben was under the impression that the old lady who owned the house died around six years ago, so I would say the person either died there or was placed there after the owner's death."

"That's creepy. And would mean that the person who put the body there knew the owner of the property?" Jack asked.

"Either that or the killer, if we can refer to them that way, knew the area well enough to know that the owner had died and the house was no longer being lived in," Lorne said.

"Both feasible," Sally said. "Until we know more about the owner's death and her family, all we can do is speculate."

* * *

IT WASN'T until nearing four that afternoon that they received a glimmer of hope. Stuart called Sally from one of the neighbours', telling her that the owner was Edna Chalmers and she had left her estate to her nephew who had moved to Australia nearly ten years earlier.

"I don't suppose the neighbour has a number for the nephew, do they?"

"Yes, I've got it here, they also gave me the name of the solicitors who dealt with the will and probate."

"So she didn't die intestate after all? Obviously, don't answer that. Okay, come back to base and we'll have a chat about anything else you managed to find out. What am I thinking? I'm really not with it today. Why don't you give me the solicitor's number I can give them a call now? I'll see what they can tell me before I ring the nephew."

"I was just about to do that, boss. Have you got a pen handy?"

She searched her desk for the pen that had got buried under her paperwork and pulled the notebook towards her. "Go on."

"The nephew's name is Charles Langdon."

Sally jotted down the numbers. "Melbourne, eh? Nice part of the world."

"So I've heard," Stuart said. "And the solicitors are Thomas and Whitley in Norwich."

"Great. Thanks, Stu. See you soon."

She rang the solicitors first and asked to speak to the person dealing with Edna Chalmers' will to see if they could give any further information about her death.

"Mitchel Thomas, how can I help, Inspector?"

"Thanks for sparing the time to speak with me, Mr Thomas. Hopefully I won't keep you too long."

"It's fine, I've finished all my client appointments for the day. What type of information were you after?"

"We're aware that the house was left to Charles Langdon. I just wondered if any other relatives benefited from the will, if so, what was the likelihood of someone—by someone, I mean that person might have a spare key to the house?"

"Hmm… let me take a look through the notes I made on the system."

Sally heard the keyboard clack and his computer beep a few times, then he cursed under his breath and came back on the line.

"Would you believe the system has just crashed? God, I

hate technology, but hey, we're stuck with it, aren't we? Let me track down the paper file."

The phone clattered. Sally got distracted by a pen stain on her desk. She licked her finger then rubbed at the stain and broke into a smile when it faded and disappeared.

"I'm back, sorry for the delay. Before I give you the information, I should have asked why you need it. Bearing in mind that Mrs Chalmers died in twenty seventeen."

"I should have told you, I apologise. We were called to the house yesterday. Are you aware that it is in dire need of repair?"

"I wasn't but I'm not surprised. Mrs Chalmers lived at the house alone for over fifty years. You were called out to the house because…?"

"Someone broke in and got more than they bargained for when they were snooping around."

"I'm intrigued, Inspector. What did they find?"

"The remains of a dead body."

He gasped and then fell silent for a while.

"Mr Thomas, are you okay?"

"I will be, which is more than can be said for the person you discovered. You mentioned remains. I take it that means that this person has been dead a while then, yes?"

"That's right, although the pathologist can't give us any indication of how long, not yet, not until she's carried out a thorough examination of the remains which may even involve bringing in further experts to help with her assessment."

"Oh dear, I don't envy the person who stumbled across the find, but there again, maybe they got their just desserts for breaking into the property."

"While on the one hand I wholeheartedly agree with you, on the other, if they hadn't discovered the remains, someone's family would still be none the wiser about their loved one."

"Yes, I understand. What a dreadful situation you find yourself in. Let me see if I can give you any information to make your job easier."

"Any help, no matter how small, I'm sure will go a long way to assist me in my unenviable task."

"What do you know about the situation so far?"

"That the house was left to Charles Langdon who lives in Melbourne, Australia. But that information was gathered from a neighbour, hence my calling you, to get clarification of the truth."

"I can understand that. Yes, it's true. When I had a telephone conversation with him, in which I broke the news about his aunt's will, he appeared to be upset and told me that he had no imminent plans to come back to the house. I proposed that he sold it. But he was determined to hang on to it because he had very fond memories of being at the house when he was a youngster. He later rang me, a couple of years had passed by then, to inform me that he had booked a flight to come over. I told him to drop by and see me at the office if he needed any further assistance. I then received a call from him to say that the pandemic had struck and all flights had been cancelled." He sighed. "As you know, it wasn't just our country that was forced to lockdown but the whole world because of that damned virus."

"Ah, yes, so it was. Has he been in touch with you since?"

"He called me a few months later, told me he was in the process of fighting the airline to get his money back, but it had gone into administration, therefore he was doubtful if he would ever get a refund from them."

"Damn, I think it must have happened a lot around that time. I have a friend who booked a wedding reception and the hotel went bust, owing her thousands. She's still going through the legal process to recover her deposit."

"Yes, my wife is also a solicitor, she's handled a few cases similar to that herself. I'm on the fence. I know these venues needed to take the deposits from couples, but surely they've had no outlay as such, we're talking eighteen months ahead. I believe a lot of places were probably up to their eyes in debt and have seen the pandemic as an answer to their prayers. It's appalling, but I suppose it's the nature of the beast when funds are low and times are bad."

"To steal from the general public? Forgive me if I don't agree with you. Those people have used their hard-earned money to place a deposit on trust and been effectively scammed because of the small print in the contract that no one bothers to read."

"Fair point. I fear we've drifted far from the original subject."

"Oops, yes, let's get back on track, my fault entirely."

"The point is, Mr Langdon hasn't been in touch with me since; therefore, I assume that funds have been near impossible to come by."

"I suppose Australians must be suffering from their own cost-of-living crisis."

"I suspect you're right. As to your other question, there were no further members of the family mentioned in the will. So, I'm assuming that I will no longer be of use to you, Inspector."

"Don't worry, I'm thankful for you sparing the time to speak with me."

"I can give you Mr Langdon's number, if you want it?"

"That would be perfect, thank you so much." Although Stuart had already passed the number on to her, she accepted it from Mr Thomas just in case the neighbour had an old number or had written it down wrongly.

He read it out, and it turned out to be a match.

"I can't thank you enough for your help, Mr Thomas. I'll give Charles a ring now."

"Umm... you might want to wait a few hours. They're either twelve hours behind us or ahead of us, I can never remember which."

"Ah, yes, that would mean it's coming up to five in the morning over there. It's no problem, I can call him when I get home this evening, at around eight."

"I'm sure that would be far more agreeable to him. Good luck with your investigation. Don't hesitate to get in touch with me if you think I can be of further assistance."

"You're very kind. Thank you."

Sally returned to the outer office to update the team. "Do we have any other information to hand about the deceased's property?"

"Like what?" Jack replied. "What else is there to dig for? You've got a contact number for the new owner of the property. Until you get to speak to him, our hands are tied on where the investigation goes next, aren't they?"

"I suppose so. Okay, if there's nothing else for us to sink our teeth into, we might as well call it an early night for a change."

"Are you feeling all right?" Jack shot back at her.

"Cheeky sod. Let's make the most of it while we can. I won't be able to speak to Charles Langdon for a few hours yet. Of course, if you don't want to go home to your beautiful wife and children, Jack, I'm sure I can find you some laborious paperwork to do in our absence."

He leapt out of his chair, slipped his arms into his jacket and was standing by the door before Sally could inhale another breath. "See you guys in the morning, I think there's a pint or two that have got my name on them down at my local."

Sally tutted and shook her head. "It's great, the way you men always put the boozer before dashing home to be with your loved ones. Why don't you give Donna a ring? Maybe she'd like to join you at the pub for a change."

Jack's eyes widened, and his head jutted forward. "That, Inspector Parker, would be sacrilege."

Sally screwed up a scrap piece of paper and aimed it at him. "Go, get out of here, you sad excuse for a human being."

"Hey, I don't need telling twice. Laters."

"Go on, you guys get on your way as well. Why should he be the only one to leave early?"

The chairs scraped, and the rest of the team switched off their computers and left the office. The only one to remain behind was Lorne.

"I'll pass. I don't mind getting stuck into that paperwork you were threatening Jack with, if you like."

Sally perched on the desk next to her best friend. "What's going on? You're usually chomping at the bit to get home to that gorgeous husband of yours."

Lorne shrugged. "I can't put my finger on it, maybe this case has got a hold of me already. You know as well as I do that some cases strike a chord more than others."

Sally rubbed Lorne's upper arm. "Hey, it's in its infancy at present. Let's make the most of it and get some rest while we're able to. Come on. Want me to drop you off on the way? I can bring you in tomorrow, too, no bother."

"Seems silly to do that. I'm fine. I'll tidy up my desk and be right behind you, I promise."

Sally knew that when Lorne had her mind set on something it would be futile trying to change it for her. "If you're sure. I'll see you in the morning then."

"Enjoy your evening."

* * *

Sally arrived home to find Dex lying in his basket in the kitchen. "Hey, you, aren't you going to come and say hello to me?"

Dex wagged his tail, but she could tell he wasn't feeling himself and she noticed his nose was dry, too.

Simon entered the kitchen behind her and kissed her on the cheek. "You're home early. Anything wrong?"

"Not with me, but it looks like Dex is feeling under the weather."

"Umm... yes, he was sick in the car this afternoon, so Tony and I decided it would be best to postpone our planned trip and bring the poorly pup home."

"Oh no, what's wrong, baby?" She crossed the vast kitchen and sat on the floor next to her beloved pet who was getting on a bit now. He was going to be ten soon, even though she still thought of him as a puppy. "Should we take him to the vet to get checked over?"

"I would leave it until tomorrow. He might have picked up a bug or eaten something dodgy on his walk."

She bounced to her feet. "Did you keep an eye on him?"

"Of course I did... most of the time."

"What do you mean?"

"I took a call from one of the builders while we were walking down by the river, and he might have gone out of sight for a second or two."

"Seriously? You know what a scavenger he can be. He needs to be supervised every second he's out and about. Did he come back to you when you called him?"

"Eventually. He disappeared behind a bush."

She ran a hand through her hair and tried to hold on to her temper. Dex had been dognapped a few years earlier. Simon was aware of the fact and had agreed to keep a watchful eye on him whenever he was in charge of walking him.

Sally inhaled a calming breath. "It doesn't matter. I'll cook him some scrambled egg to settle his tummy."

"I'm sorry, love."

Sally kissed him and walked into the pantry to collect three fresh eggs she had picked up from the local farm at the weekend. There was talk that Lorne and Tony were about to embark on building a coop and having twenty or so chickens running around in one of their paddocks next door. She'd be buying them fresh and super local in the months ahead.

"Want me to do it for you?"

"No, he's my dog, I'll nurse him back to health."

"Ouch, that was a bit mean, Sal."

She put the eggs in a bowl on the counter and raised her hands. "I'm sorry. Yes, you're right, it was uncalled for, but he's my baby, you know how much he means to me."

"I do. Go on, you sit with him, and I'll cook the eggs."

Sally relented and pulled a chair over to sit next to her four-legged friend who'd been through so much with her over the years. She sat and hung a hand down beside her, but Dex moved his head out of her reach and faced the wall. A tear slipped down her cheek at his rejection. She knew she was being foolish and should have backed away and left him to it, but her mothering, or should that be smothering, instinct held firm.

Simon presented Dex with his cooled scrambled eggs ten minutes later, but Dex wasn't interested in the slightest.

"Maybe we should leave him to get some rest," Simon suggested.

"Perhaps you're right. I have a call to Australia to make later so I think we should see about making dinner early tonight. Do you have a menu planned for this evening?"

"No, but I can easily throw together one of my special pasta dishes. What do you fancy?"

"Do we have any chicken? If so, what about chicken, honey and mustard served with either pasta or rice?"

"Sounds good to me. Why don't you try and coax Dex into the lounge with you?"

Sally glanced over at Dex and shook her head. "I think he'll be better off where he is. I'll go through and jot down some notes, unless you need a hand preparing the veggies."

"I don't, I think I can manage to chop a few onions and mushrooms." He went to the fridge and removed a bottle of white wine. "I'll pour us both a drink. It's not too early for you, is it?"

She smiled. "It's never too early for wine. Sorry for having a go at you, you didn't deserve that. You know how much Dex means to me."

"It's okay, and for the record, I think the world of him, too, otherwise I wouldn't take him with me when I visit the sites."

"I know."

They shared a kiss, and Sally took her wine through to the lounge and picked up the pen and paper she kept on the side table next to the sofa. Halfway through her chore, Dex decided to join her. He made himself comfortable by the fire, even though it wasn't lit.

"Are you feeling better, boy?"

He groaned and wagged his tail slightly.

"Good. We love you."

Simon brought their dinners in half an hour later, and they switched the news on while they ate. Sally was relieved to see there was no mention of the remains being found at the house.

"This call you have to make later, is it to do with the new investigation?" Simon asked. He placed his empty plate on the floor beside him.

"It is. It's to the current owner, the nephew of the woman who used to own the property."

"Bugger, he's not going to appreciate being told you've found remains at his house."

"I know. It's going to be a tough call to make."

"What time are you planning on calling him?"

"Around eight. There is a twelve hours' difference between us, I wouldn't want to get off on the wrong foot with him."

"Do we have time for a cuddle?"

He held his arm up, and Sally shifted in her seat and placed her head on his chest. It felt comforting to hear his heart beating.

"How did you get on today, with the exception of caring for our poorly pup?"

"We made some progress, highlighted a couple of areas that we can do some extra research on. Tony was very enthusiastic about what lies ahead of us."

"Hmm… talking of which, Lorne seemed fairly distant at work today, enough for me to wonder if everything was all right at home, between them." She sat up and looked at him. "I don't suppose Tony has said anything to you, has he?"

"Nothing at all. As far as I'm concerned, everything is hunky-dory."

She lowered her head to his chest again. "That's okay then."

Simon flicked through the channels and found a David Attenborough nature programme.

Sally drifted off to sleep for forty winks and woke up with a start. "Christ, not what I intended at all. I need to be fully alert for when I make the call."

"You will be. I'll get you a coffee."

"No, I'll do it. I'm going to nip upstairs and get changed anyway. I should have thought about it sooner but I got busy making my notes. I'll stick the kettle on and make the coffee when I come down."

THE COFFEE DID the job of stimulating her brain once more, and she was ready to make the call when the clock struck eight—that was until Simon presented her with a piece of chocolate cake and lashings of cream.

"Are you trying to make me put on weight?"

"You could still do with putting a few pounds on in my opinion. Go on, it won't hurt you. Hey, I'm just trying to spoil the girl of my dreams."

"You old softie. Living with you, I consider myself thoroughly spoilt every day of my life."

"Likewise. It's five to eight. Want me to leave you alone for half an hour so you can concentrate? I can catch up on my accounts in the office. I haven't filed anything for a few days, there's sure to be a mountain of invoices to wade through."

"You're an angel, thanks. Hopefully, I won't need that half an hour, but it would be good not to have any added distractions lingering around."

He smiled and went to leave the room; he tried taking Dex with him, but Dex was having none of it.

Sally dialled the long number. The phone rang four times once the connection had been made.

Then a man with a hoarse voice shouted, "Yes, what is it?"

"Hi, is that Charles Langdon?"

"The very man, who wants to know?"

"Sorry to interrupt you at this early hour, Mr Langdon. I'm DI Sally Parker calling from Norfolk in the UK. Do you have five minutes for a chat?"

"The UK? The police, you say? Why? What are you calling me about?"

"It's to do with the property you own here, sir, the one that used to belong to your aunt, Edna Chalmers."

"It's the only property I own in England," he corrected her. "What about it?"

"We were called out to the property last night. Someone broke into the house"

"What? Why? The last I saw of it the place was a tip. Oh God, we're not talking about squatters, are we? I hope your lot removed them. I know what a severe pain in the arse they can be to get out of a property once they're settled."

"No, it wasn't squatters, don't worry. The man's intentions were, let's just say questionable."

"I would have thought that was a given if he broke in. Go on, surprise me."

"He went there with the intention to have intimate relations with his girlfriend."

"Bloody hell. Is that what it has come down to back there in the UK? You have to break into a derelict property to get laid?"

Sally bit back the snigger threatening to erupt. "Anyway, shall we say he got more than he bargained for?"

"Meaning?"

"His girlfriend stormed out of the house, but rather than go after her, he decided to nose around upstairs, and that's when things got a bit dicey."

"He made it up the stairs, meaning they were intact, I gather?"

"They were, although I have to tell you the rest of the house is in a dubious state. He went into the main bedroom and discovered something in the bed. When he tried to get closer to have a proper look, the floor gave way and the whole bed ended up in the lounge below."

"Jesus! Is he all right? Not that I'm that concerned, he shouldn't have been in there in the first place."

"I agree. He's okay, very shaken up by the whole experience. It was what he found in the bed that disturbed him more than taking the fall."

"Right, and that was?"

"The remains of a deceased person."

"What? A dead body? No, wait, a skeleton, is that what you're telling me?"

"Yes. Do you have any idea who the person might be?"

"How should I know? I'm nearly eleven thousand miles away. Christ, you mean to tell me that someone has been living in my house without my knowledge and they've popped their clogs there?"

"We've yet to uncover the truth behind the discovery. My first port of call was to ring you, to make you aware of the situation."

"And now that you have, what do you expect me to do about it? I haven't got the funds to fly back and be interviewed by you, if that's where this is going."

"It's not. You have a right to know what is going on at your property, and it wouldn't be proper for me not to get in touch with you about it now being a suspected crime scene."

"I'm sorry, yes, you're right. I was wrong to question you about your motive. What happens now?"

"I need to know if you have any idea who this person might be. At the moment, we're scrabbling around, clueless."

"That makes two of us, I assure you. As far as I knew the house was empty. I admit, it probably isn't in the best state, but there has been little I could do about that in recent years. It's not like the house is just around the corner, is it? I promise you, I'm trying to get the funds together to travel to the UK. Hey, maybe I should just cut my losses and get in touch with a property manager over there to deal with it for me. Perhaps, in hindsight, I should have had the nous to have done it when my aunt died. I'm guilty of living in the past, clinging on to the good memories I made there as a child."

"I totally understand. So, what you're telling me is that no one else had access to the property?"

"Correct."

"Then my job is done. I won't keep you any longer."

"That's it? Are you going to keep in touch? Let me know who the person was when you finally uncover the truth."

"If that's what you want me to do, then yes, I can get in touch again after the investigation is over."

"Thank you, it would be good to know."

"Thanks for chatting with me. I hope I haven't spoilt your day too much."

"You have, but I suppose that's life these days. If I'm not dealing with getting my business back on track after the damn pandemic, I have you ringing me up out of the blue, when I haven't even had the chance to wipe the sleep out of my eyes, to tell me the one property I own back in Blighty is now a crime scene, sorry, suspected crime scene."

Sally struggled to find the appropriate words for a response. "Goodbye, Mr Langdon." She threw her mobile on the sofa beside her and rested her head back to stare at the ceiling, uncertain as to whether she had handled the call correctly or not. She always preferred dealing with incidents such as this face to face and never over the phone, but that wouldn't have been practical in this case.

Pulling herself together, she went in search of Simon. "Hello, I'm all finished. How are you doing?"

He filed a sheet of paper in a manilla folder and slammed it shut. "Me, too. As usual, your timing is impeccable. Everything all right?"

"Not really. Nothing to worry about, just me being silly. Do you want a coffee, or shall we open another bottle of wine instead?"

"The latter sounds good to me." He stood and approached her.

She held her head up and accepted the kiss she knew was coming her way.

"Thanks, I needed that. How's Dex?"

He was lying on his bed beside Simon's antique desk, his head turned away from them.

"He snuck in here about five minutes ago. He's about the same. We'll leave the door open, he can come and find us if he wants to, otherwise, we should let him rest."

"I agree."

They went back into the kitchen where Simon opened one of his special bottles of wine.

"I think I just turned that man's world upside down and left him feeling frustrated about what he can possibly do about it."

"Will he be coming over?" Simon asked.

"He told me he's been trying to get over here since he inherited the house, but the world shutting down put paid to that, and now he's doing his best to get his business back on track, like so many owners are having to do throughout the globe."

"Ah, that's understandable. We think we have it bad in this country. I suppose everywhere is the same, what with this damn war to contend with as well now."

"What a hateful world it has become. Things are changing at a drastic rate now. Before long it's going to become the survival of the fittest, and elderly folks will be in a race against time to save themselves."

Simon poured the wine and handed her a glass. "A bit dramatic, but yes, I think you might have a point. Tony and I were discussing the same thing only the other day. He mentioned that all the old sci-fi films from, say, twenty years ago might finally become a reality."

Sally shuddered at the thought. "I hope he's wrong about that, I really do. I dread to think what civilisation will become if it continues. We've had wars over the years, of course we have, but have they really affected the whole world with their devastation like this one has?"

"I'm sure there will be historians out there queuing up to tell you otherwise. The only way out of this constrictive situation would be to bump off Putin."

"I have to ask why either the SAS or the Navy SEALs from the US haven't attempted to assassinate him yet, bearing in mind how they pounced on Saddam Hussein."

"It's probably the threat of Putin hovering with his finger over the nuclear button that'll be playing a huge part in the other countries or nations holding back. Still, enough about world politics and work matters for one day, let's get back to the important stuff, sorting out where we're going to go for our summer holiday this year."

"Blimey, I hadn't even thought that far ahead. What did you have in mind?"

"Hawaii, what do you reckon?"

"Gosh, can we afford it?"

Simon rolled his eyes. "Of course we can, otherwise I wouldn't have suggested it. Are you up for it?"

"Am I? I'll start packing my suitcase in readiness today."

They both laughed.

"Fair enough. I'll pick up some brochures from the travel agent's the next time I'm passing, it'll give us a good foundation to then take our search on the internet. There are so many scammers at play out there today, I think it would be for the best if we took the old route now and again."

"Ah, right, that's the dinosaur in you at play, isn't it?"

"Not at all. Just keeping us safe. People in excitement mode about their holidays are often ripe for the picking."

"I'll give you that one." She puckered up for another kiss. "It's lovely to have something to look forward to."

"I would have suggested it before but I wasn't sure how Tony would fit in with the business. I feel confident in his abilities now to be able to leave things ticking over in his capable hands. I'll take a gander at our schedule over the next few days and get back to you with a proper date, see if it fits around your team and their annual holiday before I make the final booking, how's that?"

"Sounds very organised and very you, as usual. Just let me know. I'm sure we'll be able to work around it. I have Lorne on the team now, she can step up to the plate and be Jack's partner when I'm away."

"Good, that's sorted then." He raised a glass and chinked it against hers. "To Hawaii and to us enjoying ourselves."

Seconds later, Dex entered the kitchen and threw up in front of them.

CHAPTER 3

"So where do we start?" Jack asked the second he supplied her first cup of coffee for the day.

"Hold your horses, Mr Eager Nuts, why don't we wait until all the team are here before we get down to business?"

"Lorne's late, isn't she?"

"Only by a few minutes. I'll give her a ring, see what's going on." Sally removed her mobile from her jacket pocket and dialled the number.

A breathless Lorne answered the phone and pushed open the door to the incident room at the same time. "I'm here. Sorry, there was an accident on the way in. Admittedly, I was cutting it fine anyway, I left home later than usual," she spoke into the phone for half of her conversation then disconnected when the team all laughed at her. "Glad I've amused you all."

"Get your harassed workmate a much-needed cup of caffeine, Jack, and we'll begin," Sally ordered. "Are you okay, Lorne?"

"I will be, soon. Sorry again."

Sally waved her friend's apology away and stepped closer

to the whiteboard that she had brought up to date upon her arrival twenty minutes before. "As you can see, I rang Australia last night and spoke to the new homeowner. To say he was shocked would be an understatement."

Jack presented Lorne with her coffee, and they both took their seats.

"I bet," Lorne replied. "Could he shed any light on who the victim might be?"

"Nope, turns out he's as much in the dark as we are."

"Where do we go from here then?" Lorne asked.

"All we've got going for us is the rough time of death. We need to find out if there were any missing persons in the area six to seven years ago."

"I'm sure there will be," Jack added.

"The quicker we can source that information the better. We should all see what we can find out, whether that's talking to the Missing Person Department or trawling through the internet to see what that throws up to assist us."

"We should be able to source the information quickly, if we all get involved," Lorne agreed.

"I'll leave it with you and deal with the usual crap filling my desk first thing. Lorne, if you have a minute, I'd like a brief chat with you."

Lorne raised an eyebrow and took a sip from her coffee.

"Bring your drink with you," Sally threw over her shoulder.

Lorne joined Sally in her office and expelled a large breath as she fell into her seat. "Is this where I get my first reprimand for being late?"

"You think you deserve one? I was satisfied with your excuse, even though I travelled the same route as you this morning."

Lorne's gaze dropped to her mug. "Umm... I might have

exaggerated slightly, to save my neck. I'm sorry, I'll never do it again."

"What's going on, Lorne? The last couple of days there has been something off about you. I'm not used to treading on eggshells in your presence, but if I don't, you end up snapping my head off. Is everything all right at home?"

"Of course it is. Tony and I are as happy, if not happier, than we've ever been. It's just me."

"Tell me what's going on then. I thought our friendship meant as much to you as it does to me, and yet here you are, shutting me out."

"I'm not. We're in the middle of a busy case, and I don't want to burden you."

Sally inclined her head and gave Lorne one of her 'don't bullshit me, lady' looks. "Hardly in the middle, the case is in its infancy. Now, what gives, Lorne Warner?"

"The damn menopause, that's what gives. It's driving me round the bloody bend."

Sally sat back and laughed. "I'm sorry, I shouldn't have done that. Is that all? I thought it was something major affecting your life."

"It is. Christ, I hope you never have to deal with it. I wouldn't wish this feeling of helplessness on my worst enemy."

"Get to the doctor's, that's an order. Hang on, didn't he put you on HRT last year?"

"He did. What's the point when I feel like shit most days?"

"There you go, exaggerating again."

"All right, maybe I am a tad."

"I haven't done any research on the subject but I'm sure it's like any other illness out there. Some people's medication will always need adjusting, I don't suppose there's a 'one size fits all' for any drugs. Get yourself down to the doctor's and have it out with him. I wish I could wave a magic wand over you and make things right. The truth is, I can't."

"I will. I'll give him a call this morning."

Sally sat forward, picked up the office phone and threw it at Lorne. "Do it now before you forget."

Lorne withdrew her mobile from her pocket. "I'll use mine, I have the number in my contacts." She rang the surgery, and the automated voice told her she was number five in the queue.

Sally opened a few brown envelopes and dealt with a couple of emails while Lorne's fingers rhythmically drummed on the other side of her desk. "Have patience, patient."

"I'm trying. Ah, yes, I'd like an appointment with Doctor Carrington, please… Is that the earliest available? Okay, then it will have to do. Thanks."

Sally frowned. "When?"

"Three weeks away. How bloody ridiculous is that?"

Sally sighed. "I guess that's good, and yes, it's definitely a sign of the times."

Lorne rose from her seat. "Thanks for listening. Sorry to burden you with my problems."

"You haven't, and you're welcome. Three weeks will go quickly, stay positive until then."

"I'll try."

AFTER THE TEAM had bolted down their lunch, Joanna shared some exciting news with them. "My contact in the Missing Person Department has come back with four possible names. All female, all in their mid-thirties. Two were reported missing in twenty sixteen and the other two in twenty seventeen."

"Interesting. Can you write the names and addresses down for me, please, Joanna?"

"Already done, boss. I'll run a copy off just in case you need one."

"Great stuff. Looks like we're going to be busy over the next few days, folks. Anyone found anything on the internet?"

"Still doing the searches, boss," Stuart replied.

"Jack, Lorne and Jordan, I think we should all get out there, split the names and visit the families. Don't forget to take a photo of the rings with you." Sally collected the printed list from Joanna and ran her finger across each of the names. "Lorne, you and Jordan take the first two names, Natasha Yett and Lucy Dodds. Jack and I will visit Paula Wright's and Dana Caldwell's families. Joanna and Stuart can continue searching the net for any additional information in relation to each of the cases."

"Sounds good to me," Lorne replied. "Shall we head off now?"

"No time like the present. Maybe ring ahead, see if the next of kin are available to interview today."

Lorne picked up her phone and dialled the first number.

Sally left her to it and passed the list over to her partner. "Ring Caldwell's and Wright's next of kin for me while I finish up in the office. I'm expecting a response to an email I sent this morning about a previous case we solved. I'd like to get that settled today."

"Leave it with me."

TEN MINUTES LATER, the four of them set off.

"What type of reception did you both get?" she asked Lorne and Jack as they descended the stairs.

"I believe both of mine were suppressing their emotions," Lorne replied.

"Yeah, the two I contacted did pretty much the same," Jack said.

"We'll meet back here and compare notes in a few hours. If anything major turns up, give me a call. Take care."

The teams got in their respective cars and left the car park, taking different directions at the exit. Sally and Jack's first port of call was to the family of Paula Wright. The house was a mid-terrace, set on a small estate surrounded by fields on the outskirts of Hingham. A woman in her sixties opened the door.

"Mrs Wright? I'm DI Sally Parker, and this is my partner, whom you spoke to earlier, Jack Blackman."

"Thank you for coming out to see me. I'm longing to hear what you have to tell me, you were a bit evasive on the phone."

"I'm sorry," Jack mumbled the apology.

The woman showed them into the lounge at the rear of the property. The room was warm, the spring sunshine hitting the back of the house. The French windows overlooked a pretty courtyard garden, the few tubs breaking out in bloom.

"Won't you take a seat? Please, tell me what you know."

"I don't want to get your hopes up so I'm going to come right out and say it," Sally said, her mouth suddenly going dry. She ran her tongue over her lips. "A few days ago we discovered the remains of a body in a cottage out at Feltwell."

Mrs Wright gasped. "And you think it might be... my daughter, is that what you're telling me?"

"Possibly. The pathologist has given us an early indication that the corpse has likely been dead between six and seven years. We've matched up the Missing Person database and come up with four possible names. One of them was your daughter."

"I see." Tears bulged and seeped onto Mrs Wright's cheeks. "How can I help?"

"Did your daughter know anyone in that area? Or did she visit the area through work perhaps?"

"Maybe, she was a mobile hairdresser. At the time of her disappearance, the police didn't really take me seriously. I tried to tell them that my daughter was happy and that she wouldn't have upped and left her home, *this* home. She just wouldn't have."

"She lived with you, did she?"

"No, this is her home. I sold my own house and moved in here, so I could be close to her. I don't have anyone else, she was my world. I wasn't prepared to give up on her with a click of my fingers like your lot were."

"Did you have any contact with her the day she went missing?"

"Yes, we spoke several times a day. She usually rang me in between her appointments but neglected to that day."

"What do you suspect happened to her?" Sally sensed Jack wince beside her; he knew once she started with the probing questions that she wouldn't be able to stop herself, even if the corpse didn't turn out to be Paula Wright.

"She had a man after her. She reported it to the police, but apparently they couldn't give a toss, refused to even speak to the man."

"I'm unaware of your daughter's case. I'm sorry her cries for help were ignored by my fellow officers. Was she married at the time?"

"Ha, don't ask me about him. As soon as she went missing, he buggered off. Left the house and never came back. That's when the letters began arriving. The loan agreements he had taken out in her name against the house. I had to put the house on the market and buy it myself, there was no other way around it. Yes, he's probably out there, laughing at me, screwing around with bits of skirt here and there like he did when he was with her. He couldn't give two shits about Paula."

"What's his name?"

"Barry Knox."

"If they were married, can you tell me why Paula didn't take his name?"

"Because of her business, it would have been too much hassle to have switched everything over."

"And Barry was all right about that?"

"No, it ticked him off, but it didn't stop him taking out the loans in Paula's name. He knew every conceivable underhand trick in the book, that one."

"Where is he now? Still in the area?"

She shrugged and screwed up her nose. "I don't know and I don't care. He's never once been back here to see if Paula ever returned. I wouldn't put it past him to have killed her and dumped her body either."

"Oh my, things were really that bad between them?"

"No, they hid it well until she went missing. That's when he blurted it all out and the shit hit the fan. I could have killed him with my bare hands for taking off the way he did. Not giving a damn about Paula. Heartless prick. And no, I have no intention of apologising for my bad language."

Sally smiled. "There's really no need for you to, if that's how you feel about him. We'll do some digging."

Jack coughed. Sally faced him and raised an eyebrow. He handed her the photo of the rings.

"Ah, yes. Along with the remains we also found a couple of rings. Would you take a look, see if you recognise them as being Paula's?"

Mrs Wright reached into her handbag beside her chair

and put on a pair of spectacles. "Let me see. She had an amethyst engagement ring that she bought herself, and there was an inscription in the wedding ring of 'our love forever'. What a joke that was."

Sally's heart sank. She knew then that the rings didn't belong to Paula. "I'm sorry, I can tell you now they don't belong to your daughter."

Mrs Wright sobbed and wiped her nose on the tissue she removed from a small packet on the table beside her. "There was me getting my hopes up. I know I shouldn't say that, but it's the not knowing where she is that tears at my soul."

"I meant what I said, we'd like to help. I run a cold case team in Norfolk. Once we've solved this case, and we will, I'd like to have another look at your daughter's case, if you'll allow me to."

"That would be amazing. Thank you so much. I hope you find the family you're searching for soon. I can only imagine the range of emotions they'll be going through once they learn the truth."

"It's never easy hearing that a loved one has passed, no matter how many years that person has been missing. Here's my card. If you haven't heard from me in, say, a month, ring me, okay?"

"I will. I'll put it on my calendar."

She showed them back to the front door and bid them a tearful farewell.

"Why did you have to open your mouth back there? Why do you do that?" Jack questioned her.

"She has a right to know the truth. If we can be the ones to eventually provide her with it, then so be it. You can be such a grouchy bugger at times."

"Yeah, thanks for the compliment."

They got back in the car.

"Put yourself in her shoes," she said. "What if one of your

daughters went missing for six or seven years, wouldn't you want to know why?"

He sighed and stared out the window. "I suppose so. Ignore me."

"I intend to. Put the next address in the satnav before we fall out altogether."

"I don't have to put it in, I know where it is. Take a left at the top of the road, continue for two and a half miles, and it should be the first road you come to on the right."

"Get you. How come you know this area so well, or shouldn't I ask?"

"I used to date a girl from around this area called Felicity."

"Before or after your army days?"

"Before. We split up the minute I told her I'd joined up. She let rip at me, clobbered me several times. If I'd been a copper at the time, I would have banged her up in a cell for assault."

"Sounds to me like you had a lucky escape."

"Yeah, you're not wrong. Last I heard, she's on her fourth husband and is expecting her fifth child. Still as crazy and as volatile as ever, according to one of my mates. He knows the bloke she's married to now."

"Poor sod. Some women give the rest of us a bad name just by breathing the same air as us."

"You're not wrong there. I'm glad you're relatively sane, my working life would be hell otherwise."

Sally laughed and found it hard to stop. Jack tutted several times until she apologised.

CHAPTER 4

When they arrived, Rob Caldwell was outside, making the most of the sunshine, washing his car.

Sally introduced herself and her partner and offered up her ID for him to inspect.

"I'm almost finished here. Give me another couple of seconds then we'll talk inside."

"No bother. It's a lovely day for it today."

"Hard to keep on top of the cleaning, what with me being on the road all the time. You're lucky you caught me. I'm off on my travels again tomorrow until the end of the week." He threw the bucket of soapy water at the front of the car and ran to get the hosepipe.

Sally and Jack took a few steps back, out of reach of any accidental dousing they might receive, aware of what most people thought about the police.

With the car eventually rinsed off, Rob tidied up his bucket and sponge and gathered up the hosepipe, then announced that he was ready to speak with them. "Do you want a cuppa? I'm going to make myself one."

"Thanks, two coffees would be great, milk and one sugar," Sally replied with a smile.

He walked around the side of the house. They followed him through the back gate and entered the door at the rear which led into a vast kitchen-diner that Sally surmised had been recently updated.

"Take a seat. I'll put the kettle on."

They sat at the large glass dining table, and Sally admired the view of the neatly presented garden through the patio doors.

"Who's the gardener, or do you get someone in, what with you being on the road all the time?"

"My girlfriend, Abby. It's her greatest passion. Me, I don't know a rose from a dandelion, and no, I'm not joking."

"She certainly knows her stuff, it looks wonderful."

"I'll pass on the compliment. She won't even let me loose with the lawnmower, insists the garden is her baby and warns me not to interfere."

"She really is a keen gardener if she tells you that. We have a large garden, but neither of us, my husband nor I, have a clue what to do with it. We have a gardener come in every other week to keep it in shape. Have you been here long?"

"Around ten years. It was Dana, my wife's, idea to move here. I had extreme doubts in the beginning, but she managed to talk me around. She also loved gardening." He fell silent and poured milk into three mugs and added a spoonful of sugar to each of them. The kettle switched itself off. He topped up the mugs with water and then delivered them to the table; he slid two in front of Sally and Jack.

"Thanks," they replied in unison.

Rob sat opposite them and wrapped his hands around his mug. "You might as well get on with it. You mentioned on the phone this was about my wife, what about her?"

"Possibly. Here's the deal. We discovered the remains of a body a few days ago. We're trying to track down the family members of the deceased."

"And you think it could be my wife? What's led you to that conclusion, if you don't mind me asking?"

"The pathologist who analysed the remains gave us a rough idea of the time of death, between six and seven years ago. We checked through the system and found only four people had gone missing in the area around that time. One of them was your wife."

"Oh, right. And what if the person wasn't from around this area, what then?"

"Then we need to go back to the drawing board and reassess things. Umm… the thing is, we found two rings on the remains, a wedding and an engagement ring."

His gaze rose from his mug and latched on to Sally's. She slid the photo of the rings across the table and watched for his reaction. He closed his eyes and shook his head.

"I can't believe it, after all these years."

"Are you telling me that you recognise the rings, Rob?"

Tears formed in his eyes. "Yes, they were Dana's." He gulped and wiped his eyes on the sleeve of his T-shirt. "Oh God, you're not going to arrest me, are you?"

"Why would you think that?"

"Because it's what you lot do, arrest innocent people. Back then, when she first went missing, the bastard dealing with the case took me to the station and interviewed me under caution, thinking that I had done away with Dana. When I questioned why he thought that, he took great pleasure in pointing out that I was a travelling salesman and that I covered a vast area, so I had the means and capabilities to dump a body hundreds of miles away from my home. As if I would do such a thing. That man almost drove me to having a breakdown. I was teetering on the edge when I found out she'd gone missing, and it was as though he was stood behind me, on the edge of an abyss, ready to jab me with a stick, urging me to take the plunge."

"I'm so sorry you were made to suffer in that way. Can you tell me how Dana went missing?"

"The truth is, I don't know. One minute I could reach her by phone and the next I couldn't. I was away up in Newcastle at a sales conference at the time. And despite me having an alibi and presenting witness statements aplenty, that bastard still reckoned I had something to do with Dana's disappearance. If he'd spent more time trying to find the real culprit instead of hounding me, maybe she would still be alive today. Now you're telling me you think you've found her..." He shook his head and stared at the rings, then ran his hands over the photo. "We picked them out together. Back in the day, we did everything together."

Sally was eager to return to her previous question. She prompted him, "Did Dana go missing during the day or at night?"

Rob hesitated for an instant, his gaze still fixed on the rings. "In the evening." He inhaled a few large breaths and then continued, "She was out with friends at the time. They said goodnight at the end of the night—correction, in the early hours of the morning—they all went their separate ways, and I never heard from her again."

"I don't suppose you have a list of those friends, do you?"

"Six years have passed since then. I've kind of moved on, although sometimes I wonder if that's the case up here." He tapped his temple.

"I see. How long have you been with Abby?"

"Four years. She was a good friend of Dana's and was a great source of comfort to me back around the time Dana went missing."

"Was Abby out with Dana the evening she went missing?"

His head rose, and he clicked his thumb and forefinger together. "Yes, she was. She'll be able to tell you who else was there that night. Do you want me to give her a call so you can speak with her?"

"Is she at work?"

"Yes, she works in a beauty salon. They're usually quiet during the week, I'm sure she won't mind."

"Thanks, that would be great."

He left the table and went in search of his phone. Finding it on the worktop near the back door, he punched in a number. "Hi, love. Are you busy…? Good, I've got the police here, I was wondering if you would have a word with them about the night Dana went missing… yes, I think they've found her… now, don't go getting yourself all upset… I'll put Inspector Parker on the line. Sweetheart, are you all right?"

He wandered back to the table, fresh tears welling up, and handed the phone to Sally. "She's upset. Be gentle with her," he warned.

"Don't worry. Hello, Abby. Thank you for agreeing to speak with me today. I'm sorry it's under such sad circumstances."

Abby sobbed and whispered, "Is it truly her?"

"We've yet to formally identify the body, but Rob has told me the rings found with the remains are those belonging to Dana."

"Oh my… after all these years, I can't believe what I'm hearing."

"Rob told me that you were with Dana the night she disappeared, is that correct?"

"Yes, we'd been out celebrating one of our friends' birthday and we believe someone kidnapped her while she was walking home that night."

"Walking home? What time was this?"

"At one in the morning. We always walked home,

usually split up in different directions. None of us wanted to waste money on getting a cab home, and our partners were all tucked up in bed and would have hit the roof if we'd called them, except Rob, of course, who was away at the time. Sorry, I can't remember where, it was at a sales conference."

"In Newcastle, yes, he's just told us."

"That's right. I should have remembered. This has come as a total shock to me, please forgive me if I'm not thinking straight."

"Take your time. I'm going to ask you some questions about that night. Please do your best to answer them as well as you can."

"Okay, I'll try."

"I'm going to need a list of the people you were with that night, do you think you'll be able to supply one?"

"I think so. It might take a few minutes. Usually it was a regular bunch of us, but I remember there were a few of Kathryn's friends from work who joined us that evening, too."

"Whose birthday was it?"

"Kathryn Fox."

"Ah, okay." Sally had her pad and pen ready to jot down the names as Abby said them. "In your own time."

"There was me, Kathryn, Jill and Pat, who came with Kathryn, they work with her at the hairdressing salon in town."

"Do you have the name of the salon?"

"A Cut Above the Rest."

"Great. Who else was there?"

"Liz Baddock, Claire Sams, Maria Adams, Emma Taylor, who is Dana's sister, or should that be *was*?"

"Don't worry about that for now. Anyone else you can think of?"

"No, that was it. I can give you phone numbers for most of them, all but Kathryn's friends, if it will help."

"That would be great, if you wouldn't mind?"

"Let me get my address book."

Sally waited patiently for the young woman to return. "Jesus, I still can't believe what's happened. Do her parents know?"

"Not yet, that will be our next stop. We needed to get some form of identification first before we visit the family. Rob has confirmed the rings belonged to Dana, so that means our investigation can begin in earnest now."

"Oh God, can I ask where you found her? Or aren't you allowed to tell me?"

"In an abandoned house close to Thetford Forest."

"Wow, all that way. I wonder who took her and what their intentions were. Is Rob all right? I know we've been together for years but I'm also aware how deep his love was for Dana. We hadn't intended getting together, if that's what you're thinking. We needed each other. We were both really distraught at the time and needed each other's comfort to get through it. We didn't get together properly, not for a couple of years after Dana went missing."

"I understand. I believe Rob's dealing with it the best he can."

Abby fired the names and contact numbers off for Sally to note down and then sighed. "She was a very dear friend to all of us. Always a great listener."

"Did she mention at the time if she had any issues? Someone pestering her, that sort of thing?"

"No, not as far as I can remember. She was also a hairdresser, although at a different salon to Kathryn, that's how they first met, and as friends, we welcomed Kathryn into the fold. Dana was the type who could look after herself. She wasn't one of these hopeless women who couldn't stand up for themselves. That's why we all had trouble believing that something bad must have happened to her."

Sally opened the back door and stepped out onto the patio to ask her next question. "What was their marriage like?"

"Gosh, don't put me in that position, please."

"I'm sorry, it would be remiss of me not to ask."

"I know you have to. Most of the time it was great. Saying that, Dana hated that Rob was out on the road all the time."

"But you're okay with it?"

"Yes, most of the time. I think it winds me up more in the winter months. But I have a great social life with my friends. They rally around to ensure I never get lonely. Which is what we tried to do with Dana, back in the day."

"I get that. Can you tell me a bit more about that evening, if you would?"

"Like where did we go, that sort of thing?"

"Yes. I take it you ended up in a club at that time of the morning."

"That's right. The Blue Parrot, it's since closed down. I think a lot of the hospitality venues in the area struggled to find their feet after the pandemic."

"Yes, you're right. And before you ended up there?"

"We went to several of the pubs in town. The Old Ship Inn, then moved on to The Spotted Cow, then made our drunken way to The Blue Parrot. That makes us out to sound really bad, but it was a special occasion, being Kathryn's birthday. We weren't usually out every week on a pub crawl, I promise."

Sally laughed. "Would it matter if you were? Each to their own. Perhaps you can tell me what happened when you left the club that night."

"We all started walking in a group together. Wait, casting my mind back, there was a group of lads, or should I say men, wolf-whistling at us. We giggled and brushed it off, never thought anything more of it. We were in a well-lit area at the time so felt we were safe enough. No, that's wrong to say that, we didn't feel threatened by the men at all, we could handle ourselves, most of us."

"So there were no further issues with the men?" Sally made her way back inside the house again.

Jack and Rob stared at her as she entered the back door. She smiled.

"No, not that I can recall. Then we split up. We never walked home alone, always in pairs at least."

"Wait, are you telling me that someone walked home with Dana that evening?"

"Yes, hang on, let me think about this for a second. That's right, Maria Adams walked most of the way with her."

"Most of the way?"

"Yes, she stopped behind a bush to have a wee and told Dana to go on ahead. They lived a few streets from one another, you see."

"Ah, okay. I'll chase that up when I speak with her. Our first stop will have to be breaking the news to Dana's immediate family."

"I don't envy you that task. They were very close. I know they fell out with Rob years ago, once that bastard of a policeman accused Rob of having something to do with his wife's death, or disappearance at the time, even though the copper didn't have any evidence to back up his claims."

"Sounds a shambolic way to run an investigation. I'll be looking into it, I assure you."

"Good. People like that, with an obvious agenda, shouldn't be allowed in the force. I got the impression he was the type to let the power go to his head."

"I'll be delving into the case more upon my return to the station, now that we've identified who the remains belong to, well, presumably. We'll have to wait for the pathologist to sign off on that really."

"I'm in two minds what to think now. I'm pleased she's been found, if it is her, but also devastated that we've all lost our dear friend at the same time. Lord knows what emotions Rob is going through at the moment. Can I have another word with him, if you've asked all the questions you needed to ask?"

"Of course. I appreciate all the information you've given me. I'm sure it's going to be a massive help with the investigation."

"My pleasure. I hope you find out what happened to Dana. It would be cruel to come this far and to never find out the truth."

"We'll do our very best, I promise. Here's Rob now." Sally smiled and handed the phone back to Rob whose hand shook when he took it from her.

"Hi, love. How did you get on with the inspector…? Yes, she seems nice, they both do. I'm all right, don't worry about me… Okay, I'll see you later. We'll raise a glass to Dana's memory, eh…? Aww… I didn't mean to make you cry. Love you." He ended the call and sniffed. "God, I've started her off again. Why is this so hard to take? I thought I'd be relieved the day someone walked in here and told me they'd recovered her body, but the opposite is true. I just don't know how or what to think about it all. My greatest fear is that it's going to open up a can of worms that will lead you back here to my door. I swear, I had nothing to do with my wife's death and I have major regrets of ever leaving her alone that week, but it was out of necessity. To increase sales, to make our lives better. A lot of good that did me, us, eh?"

"Don't worry. I believe you. I'll check through the original notes, and if there is anything in there that shouldn't belong there, I'll fight to get it removed."

"Thank you, Inspector. That's good to know."

"One last thing before we go… Can you give me Dana's parents' address, and phone number, if you have it?"

"Sorry, I deleted their phone number years ago when they refused to have anything more to do with me. But their address is fifteen Forsythe Avenue, Old Buckenham, at least it used to be, when I last visited them."

"That's great, we'll shoot around there now to share the news with them."

"Even though they turned their backs on me when I needed them the most, my heart goes out to them."

"I'll pass on that message, if you want me to?"

"I wouldn't bother. They believe me to be the Devil reincarnated."

Sally couldn't help but feel sorry for the man. She smoothed a hand up and down his arm. "I'm sure things will turn out for the best, once they realise you weren't involved in her death."

"I'd like to believe that but I doubt if it will happen."

"We'll see, never lose hope."

He smiled and shook her hand.

Back in the car, Jack tutted.

"What's that for?" She queried and started the engine.

"Why dismiss him altogether? What if the parents are right and he had a hand in her murder? We don't know anything to the contrary yet. I couldn't believe what I was hearing back there."

Sally pulled away from the kerb and let out a sigh. "I'm going by my gut feeling, and no, it's never let me down in the past, as you know."

"That's as may be, but why tell him that? I would have played it cool back there, instead, you've laid your cards on the table and dismissed any type of involvement. What if he paid someone to get rid of her? Yes, he had an alibi, but it's not beyond his realms to have sent someone to get rid of her while he was away."

"How many times have we dealt with scenarios of that ilk in the past, Jack? None that I can think of. Maybe you've been watching too many American cop shows and it's having a major impact on your judgement."

Out of her peripheral vision she saw him fold his arms and sink lower into his seat. "Whatever. Don't come running to me if all this blows up in your face."

"Hey, don't worry. As you know, I live and die by the decisions I make in my professional and personal life, always have done and always will do. Nothing anyone wants to fling at me will alter that either. Now, do something useful and put the address in the satnav, unless you know where they live?"

He muttered something indecipherable and sat forward to input the information, then with a huff, resumed his position. Sally swallowed down the snigger threatening to emerge.

En route, she rang the other team. "Lorne, just a heads-up, we believe we've identified the remains."

"Oh right, and here we were, dreading going back to the station and telling you that we had drawn a blank. That's a relief. Who is she?"

"Rob Caldwell recognised the rings as belonging to his wife, Dana."

"Ah, okay. I suppose that's a no-brainer then. Shall we head back to base?"

"Yeah, we've got a list of people we need to see. I doubt if we'll be back until later this afternoon."

"What about splitting the list up again?" Lorne suggested.

"No, I think it would be better if one team sticks to the job, that way, we can tackle any queries about differences in the witnesses' stories as they come up, if you get my drift?"

"I do. Fair enough. Anything you want us to do?"

"You can bring up the original details of the investigation and start ploughing through that for any inconsistencies. Apparently, Rob Caldwell was the main suspect at one point. He was arrested but later released because no body was ever found, even though he'd been away all week at a sales conference."

"Ouch. Could he have paid someone to have kidnapped his wife?"

"After speaking with him, my gut is telling me no, but what do I know? We're on our way to break the news to the parents. They fell out with Rob once the SIO arrested him."

"That's tough, if he's an innocent party in all of this. Okay, see you when you get back. We'll pull up the case and see what else we can find out before you return."

"Cheers, Lorne. TTFN."

CHAPTER 5

They pulled up outside the small detached cottage fifteen minutes later.

"This is quaint," Sally said. "You don't really see too many thatches nowadays."

"I've seen plenty. Wouldn't give them the time of day. The fire risk sends the insurance premiums through the roof. If you'll excuse the pun, it wasn't intentional, I assure you."

"Get over yourself, Jack. You made a funny, why don't you crack that miserable face of yours and be done with it?"

"As I said, it wasn't intentional."

"Come on, misery guts, let's see if her parents are at home."

"There's a Merc sitting on the drive, odds are that someone is in."

Sally had already spotted the vehicle, so she didn't bother replying to his observation. Instead, she got out of the car and made her way towards the front door. With her warrant card in her left hand, she rattled the knocker with her right. Jack appeared beside her just as the door was answered by a woman in her sixties wearing a nurse's uniform.

"Hello, can I help?"

Sally showed her ID and said, "Hello, Mrs Taylor. I'm DI Sally Parker of the Norfolk Constabulary, and this is my partner, DS Jack Blackman. Would it be all right if we came in and had a word with you?"

The woman's brow knitted, and her feet shuffled nervously. "May I ask what this is about?"

"We have some news regarding your daughter's disappearance, Mrs Taylor."

She staggered and fell against the door. "Oh my... I knew this day would come. I just never knew when. Come in. I'm sorry for overreacting."

Sally smiled and stepped over the threshold and into the hallway. "There's really no need for you to apologise. I don't suppose your husband is home, is he?"

"He is. I'm his carer. He had a debilitating stroke not long after Dana went missing. I've always considered it was because of the stress. I'm a part-time nurse at a home up the road as well. A carer comes in twice a week to care for him, to cover the shifts I do at the home. It gives my husband and I both the break we need to be able to cope with what life has thrown at us. Just to warn you, I will need to go soon, in about twenty minutes. Yvonne will be here shortly as well."

"It's okay, we won't take up much of your time."

"Come through to the lounge. You're lucky, I've done the housework this morning."

The scent of orange hit Sally as soon as she entered the room. "It smells lovely in here."

"Thank you. I finally got around to polishing all the wood with Orange Glo, have you tried it?"

"I haven't, but I'll definitely look it up."

"Take a seat. Forgive me for being a tad confused, for you to show up at my door after all these years without any contact... oh God, am I right in thinking that you have some devastating news for me?"

Bile burned Sally's throat. It was always the same in instances such as this, when ruining a parent's life forever was on the cards. "I'm sorry, but yes, we have reason to believe we have found your daughter's body."

"How? Where?" she asked, staring at Sally, stunned. There were no tears, not at this stage. Her hands clenched and unclenched in her lap, though.

"In an abandoned house, close to Thetford Forest."

Mrs Taylor sucked in a few deep breaths before she replied. "Was she intact? I don't really know how else to ask that question, please forgive me."

"It's okay. What we believe are her remains were found, maybe I should have mentioned that in the first place."

Mrs Taylor covered her face with her hands and cried. Pieces of Sally's heart chipped away at the sight of the broken woman. She moved towards her to offer her comfort, knowing that it was beyond her husband's realms to do it.

"Can I get you anything? A tissue, a cup of tea?"

"No, I'll be fine, once the news has sunk in. I should ring my children, they need to be here. Would that be okay?"

"Of course, whatever you need to do is fine by me."

"Oh no, I need to call work first, let them know I won't be in today."

"Would you like me to do that for you? To ease the burden on your shoulders a little."

"I'll get the number, thank you." She nipped out of the room and returned with her mobile a few seconds later. She'd not long sat down again when the doorbell rang. "Oh heck, that will be Yvonne. I'll let her in."

"You stay there, my partner can do it. Do you want to see her or should he send her away?"

"No, she can come in, she generally sits in the bedroom

with Barry while she's here anyway. It'll free up my time to share the news with my children."

"Jack, can you do the honours? Thanks."

Jack left the room and returned to inform them that Yvonne said to call her if she was needed.

Sally rang the nursing home where Mrs Taylor worked and told them she'd had some unexpected news and that she wouldn't be able to make it into work. The woman on the other end sounded off-hand, but Sally wasn't about to argue with her. She stated her reason for calling and hung up.

Mrs Taylor was on the phone to her daughter. It was impossible for her to hold back the tears. "Emma, please, I don't want to discuss it over the phone, love. I need you to come home, right away... You will...? Okay, I'll see you soon. Drive carefully... Yes, I'm going to call him now."

She ended the call and immediately made another one. "Michael, it's me. Sorry to interrupt you during the day, but I need you to come home right away... please, trust me, don't ask, just come home... okay, I'll see you shortly... thank you for trusting me. Drive safely."

Mrs Taylor threw the phone on the couch beside her and buried her head in her hands once more. Moments later, she sat upright and pushed her shoulders back. "I need to put the kettle on, they'll both be here soon, and poor Yvonne will be wanting a drink, too."

"I can do it, it's no bother," Sally offered. She rose to her feet.

Mrs Taylor did the same, but her legs gave way beneath her.

"Oh my, I can't even stand up properly. How am I going to cope? This is the nightmare I've been waiting years to happen. Our lives will change from this day forward forever."

"I can arrange for counselling for you and your family.

You're never alone, I promise. Let me make the drinks, you stay there."

"I need to check on Yvonne. Let her know what's going on, but then, I don't want Barry overhearing the conversation, it could do him untold damage if he heard upsetting news. God, this is such a mess. Why now? Why after all these years? I know that sounds a silly question, I don't really expect you to answer it."

"I'll do my best to answer any questions you and your children have when they arrive. For now, I'll prepare the drinks." Sally left her partner to take up the slack in the lounge while she breezed through the house and into the kitchen. She prepared seven mugs with milk just in case Mr Taylor wanted a drink as well. The kettle was old and took an eternity to boil. Sally used the time to rehearse what she wanted to say to the family, once the children arrived.

A woman in her forties wearing jeans appeared in the doorway. "Oh, sorry, I thought you were Jane. Who are you?"

"I'm Sally. Are you Yvonne?"

"Yes, that's right. Barry is a little agitated, he must sense there is something going on around here."

"I'll get Jane to come in and comfort him. I was going to make a drink; do you and Barry want one?"

"Yes, two teas, one with no sugar, that's mine." She collected a beaker off the draining board. "This is Barry's, it's safer for him to drink out of this."

"Ah, I did wonder. No problem. Let me go and see if Jane is up to seeing her husband." Sally sped through the hallway and into the lounge. "Sorry, Jane, Yvonne came in the kitchen and mentioned that Barry seems a little agitated, are you all right to check on him?"

She stood and tore towards Sally. "Oh yes, I need to be with him." Surprisingly, her legs managed to hold up during her journey to the downstairs bedroom along the hallway.

"Anything I can do?" Jack asked. "I feel like a spare part just sitting here."

"Come into the kitchen with me then. The other members of the family should be here soon."

They hadn't been in the kitchen long when the kettle boiled, but Sally held off from making the drinks.

The front door opened, and a male voice called out, "Mum."

Sally went into the hallway and was greeted by a man in his thirties. "Is it Michael?"

"That's right. Where is she?"

"Dealing with your father. She won't be long."

He nodded and went into the lounge. A few minutes later, the front door opened and closed again, and a young woman with large-rimmed glasses came into the kitchen.

"Oh, you're not Mum, is she around?"

"She's in with your father. Are you Emma? I'm just about to make a drink. Do you and your brother have tea or coffee?"

"Yes, that's right. Both coffee, one sugar and milk in one of them. Where's Mike?"

"In the lounge. I'll be in soon."

Emma turned on her heel, her long black hair swaying rhythmically as she moved.

Jack stared at Sally and shrugged. "Good luck with what you're about to tell them, they both seem really uptight to me."

"Gee, thanks. Nothing like making me feel ten times worse and full of trepidation."

He grinned. "You're most welcome. Can I take some of those?"

"Two coffees, one with and one without, don't mess them up."

"As if I would." Jack left the kitchen and returned a few moments later to collect two more coffees.

"I'll deliver these to Yvonne and join you in a sec. Don't say anything until I get there."

"So you expect me to stare into space, ignoring them?"

"Why not? It's what you usually do."

"As if," he grumbled.

Sally knocked on the door up the hallway, and Yvonne collected the two drinks from Sally.

"He's almost there now, Jane will join you in a moment."

"Thanks." Sally smiled and inhaled a breath then opened the door to the lounge. "Hello, again. Your mother won't be long now. Thank you both for coming here today to support her."

"Are you going to tell us what's going on?" Michael demanded. He placed his mug on the coffee table and crossed his arms.

"All in good time."

"You realise both of us were working and had to leave our jobs to get here. You're lucky we both work locally."

"I'm grateful for you both for coming." Sally fell silent until their mother came into the room.

Jane rushed towards her children and collapsed into their outstretched arms.

"What is it, Mum?" Emma asked.

"She's been found," Jane choked out.

"No," Emma shouted. "After all this time?"

"No way. Where?" Michael demanded, his question aimed at Sally.

"Why don't we all take a seat, and I'll run through how and what happened?"

The three of them released each other and sat side by side on the leather sofa, each of the children clutching their mother's hands.

"She was discovered in an abandoned house, close to the forest."

"How? Do you know who put her there? How long has she been there? Was she held there and tortured?" Michael asked.

Sally glanced his way. "They're all sensible and obvious questions. The truth of the matter is that I can't answer them. We're at the preliminary stages of the investigation, and to be honest with you, we only found out the remains might belong to your sister barely an hour ago."

"How?" Emma asked.

"Your sister's name appeared on a missing persons list from twenty sixteen and seventeen. Once the remains were found, the pathologist gave us those dates to work with. My partner and I visited Rob earlier, and he confirmed that a pair of rings found on the corpse belonged to Dana."

Jane broke down again, and Michael bounced to his feet.

"He's done this to her. He's the one who killed her. I hope you've arrested him," he said, his voice rising through the octaves, his outrage evident.

Sally held up a hand. "We still have a lot of investigating to do yet. I have to plough through the original files regarding her missing person case." She held back from telling them that she believed Rob when he'd told her that he wasn't involved in either his wife's disappearance or her death. "He's given me, or should I say, Abby provided me with a list of friends Dana was out with that night. I'll be speaking to all of them over the next few days."

"You were there, Emma, weren't you?" Michael turned to face his sister.

Emma closed her eyes and nodded. "I was. All of us were devastated when we heard that Dana had gone missing the following day."

"Can we have a private word?" Sally asked.

Emma's eyes opened, and her gaze flitted between her brother and her mother. "I can talk in front of my family. We all had a blast that evening and at the end of it drifted off in different directions, never thinking that would be our final evening together as a group."

"Was she drunk?"

"Not really. I suppose you would have classed her as being a bit merry, but she had her wits about her. None of us would have let our guard down that much, aware of how unsafe the world had become towards women, even in those days."

"Why didn't you get a damn taxi home, like I told you to?" Michael snapped.

"Because they're robbing bastards. You don't know what it's like to be a vulnerable woman in a cab. They find every which way they can to rip us off, intentionally taking the wrong route to get extra money out of us. Either that or half the time coming on to us, trying to get a cheap thrill in the back of the cab."

"Really?" Sally asked. "Men like that should always be reported to the council. Their licence would be stripped within days."

Emma shook her head. "Most women can't be bothered with all the hassle that entails. So the alternative seemed a good idea at the time."

"It will never make sense to me, never," Michael said. He threw himself back onto the sofa and stared at his distraught sister.

"Don't start, Michael," his mother warned. "We thrashed out the whys and wherefores at the time. There's no point in us going over old ground."

"Isn't there?" he replied stubbornly. "Women need to take more responsibility for their actions late at night."

Sally cleared her throat. "I don't believe that's right.

Women have just as much right to walk the streets at night as men do. Why should they be punished for letting their guard down?"

"I uh, I… oh, all right," he conceded. "If you put it that way. But, even as a bloke, when I'm out there late at night, which isn't often, I'm still constantly looking around me, just in case anyone jumps me, you know, to rob me. Why shouldn't women feel the same way?"

"There are always two sides to every argument, I'll grant you that," Sally admitted, "however, women still have the right to walk the streets safely without the fear of someone attacking, or in your sister's case, killing them."

The room fell silent, interrupted only by Jane's intermittent sobs.

"Is there anything else you can tell me? Anything you can think of that you thought strange around the time of Dana's disappearance?"

The family members all looked at each other and shook their heads.

"No, I can't think of anything," Emma said, her voice now barely above a whisper.

"I want to know what happens next," Michael stated.

"We'll take the information we've gathered back to the pathologist. She'll request Dana's dental records. If you can recall who her dentist was, that will be a great help."

"I think she went to the same one as me. Thorpe's Dental Practice," Emma replied.

"Great, thanks."

"What then?" Michael asked. He was like a dog with a bone.

"Once any possible DNA and dental records have been matched, then Dana's remains will be sent to a funeral home and you'll be able to lay her to rest, although that might take some time while the investigation continues."

"At last," Jane said. She wiped her eyes with a fresh tissue. "I've waited so long for this day to arrive, now it's here, I don't know how to feel about it."

"It'll get easier, Mum. We need to make sure it's her yet," Michael said. "How long will it be before we have the confirmation?"

"If you have doubts that Rob might be mistaken, I can show you the photo of the rings."

Michael held out his hand. Sally slipped the photo into it.

He stared at it for a few seconds and then showed it to his mother and sister. "They look like hers to me, Mum?"

"Yes, I'm sure of it. That engagement ring is a unique design. I don't mean that Rob commissioned it especially for Dana, but I don't see many of them around like that."

Sally accepted the photo back from Michael.

"You should still investigate his role in her disappearance," he said. "Don't you think it was a massive coincidence that Dana should go missing while he was away for the week? I do, and I did back then, too. I've always had my suspicions about that bloke. Your lot should have finished the job off, charged him for her murder and been done with it. At least we would have had some form of closure."

"He couldn't have been charged. By all accounts, his alibi checked out and was corroborated by several witnesses. Furthermore, steps are rarely taken in such cases without a body."

"It's wrong, because I feel it in the depths of my soul that he's a hundred percent guilty and he's been able to get away with it all these years. It'll be interesting to see what his reaction is going to be now that you believe you've discovered Dana's body. I hope you'll be keeping a watchful eye on him in the coming days and weeks."

"We will. I guarantee you that my team and I won't rest until we've uncovered the reason behind Dana's death and who the culprit is. However, I have a word of caution for you, Michael."

He crossed his arms again. "Oh yeah, and what's that?"

"That you allow us to carry out our jobs and hold back from taking the law into your own hands."

His mother grasped his arm. "Oh my, he wouldn't do that, would you, Michael?"

Avoiding eye contact with Jane, he shook his head. "No, but don't think the thought hasn't crossed my mind now and again."

"At the risk of repeating myself, we have no evidence at all that Rob was involved, none that has come to light as yet, but it's still early days. I'm going to have to ask you to have faith in my team. We have dozens of cold cases under our belts and have managed to convict several guilty parties so far. Just give us a chance to collate the evidence. Will you do that, Michael?"

"And if I'm not prepared to do that?" he bit back.

"Then Rob isn't the only one we'll be keeping an eye on over the next few weeks."

His eyes narrowed. "Is that a threat?" he countered.

"I'm not in the habit of making threats, sir. If there's nothing else you can add then we'll make a move and get started on the investigation."

"Yes, I think it would be wiser if you left the house now," Michael agreed, his gaze boring into Sally's soul.

Jack stood and took a few steps forwards. "Let us do our job, sir. I get a sense from your reaction that you're going to have trouble accepting that we're prepared to do our best for this family."

Michael went to stand, but his mother grabbed his arm.

"Behave, Michael, don't you think I'm going through enough turmoil at the moment? I can do without all this unnecessary angst."

"Sorry, Mum. All I'm trying to do is ensure these two do their jobs properly and deliver us the results we want, quickly."

"And I've assured you that will be the case, Michael, just give us a chance," Sally said. "The body was only discovered a few days ago, and here we are today, giving you our initial findings. I needn't have included you in the investigation but I felt I must, so, all I'm asking is that you give us a chance, for now."

"She's right, Mike," Emma said. "I trust her, you should do the same."

He said nothing further, only shrugged.

"I'll leave you a couple of cards. If you think of anything pertaining to the case that you believe I should know about, please do get in touch." She handed the cards to Emma.

"Thanks, we will. Do your best for us, for Dana," Emma whispered.

"You have my word. Take care of each other."

Sally and Jack left the house.

"I was getting ready to bop him one on the nose in there," Jack muttered as they made their way back to the car.

"And you would have had me to deal with if you had. Now and again, you need to take a step back, assess the situation for what it is instead of getting all hot-headed about it. That family must be going through a tornado full of emotions right now, we have to accept taking a bit of flack on the odd occasion."

"Consider me told. Makes no odds to me to take a step back. At the end of the day, all I was trying to do was protect you. Maybe I should think twice about doing that in the future."

"The last thing I want to do is fall out about this, Jack. As you know, I'm more than capable of looking out for myself."

He chose not to retort, and they both got in the car.

"Where to now?" he asked.

"I think we should start working our way through the friends' list, see if anything else comes to light about what was going on in Dana's life back then."

"Joy of joys. How to bore the pants off me with one small sentence."

"Shut up moaning and put the first address in the satnav."

"And what if these people aren't at home during the day?"

"All right, smart arse. You've got their phone numbers, give them a call. Who's up first?"

"Maria Adams." He removed his mobile from his pocket and dialled the number. "Yes, Miss Adams, this is DS Jack Blackman. I was wondering if it would be convenient to drop by and have a brief chat with you… Now, preferably… at work, if possible… I've got that, thanks, we'll see you in around twenty minutes. Goodbye."

He ended the call, and Sally turned to look at him.

"Well? Where am I heading? It would help to know, if we have any intention of getting to the location."

"Blimey, give me a chance. I'll put it in now. She works at a haulage firm on the outskirts of Attleborough."

"I'll head in that direction for now then. In your own time, partner."

CHAPTER 6

*I*t was an active time of the day at the haulage firm. Three lorries were on their way out of the yard as Sally indicated to enter the car park.

"Busy place. Didn't know this was here, did you?"

"Yep, my mate used to work for them, a few years back. That reminds me, I need to catch up with Alan soon, he owes me a tenner. I'll get interest off him in the form of a pint, it's what we do."

Jack laughed, and Sally shook her head.

"Men!"

Sally parked in the closest spot to the office she could find. They entered the building and were greeted by a petite female with a striking red mane of hair.

She left her desk and approached the counter. "Hi, how can I help you today?"

Sally nudged Jack to take the lead as he had spoken to the young woman on the phone already.

He produced his warrant card. "DS Blackman. Are you Maria Adams?"

She smiled and tutted. "Of course you are. Sorry, I was

miles away for a second there. Lots of schedules to keep up with today. Everything is a bit of a whir. What can I do for you? Wait, can I get you a drink?"

"No, we're fine, thanks. This is my boss, DI Sally Parker. She'll take it from here."

Sally suppressed a giggle at her partner's insistence to keep out of the limelight, as usual.

"Oh, pleased to meet you. You didn't say, and I forgot to ask over the phone, what's all this about?"

"Are we free to talk quietly here? Or is there somewhere else we can go where we won't be disturbed?"

"Here's fine. The last of the men are due to leave the yard soon. I'll just wave them off. The boss is out, drumming up extra business, so we shouldn't be disturbed. We don't tend to get many people walk in off the street." She lifted the flap in the counter and invited them to join her. "I'll get another chair."

"Tell me where to find it and I'll get it," Jack offered.

"Pop your head round that door, there should be one in there on the right. I don't think the boss would appreciate his executive chair being wheeled out here."

Jack found a plastic chair and slotted it alongside Sally's. "This will do, thanks." He flipped open his notebook and poised his pen over an empty page.

"Okay, first off, I have to tell you that we've reopened the investigation into the disappearance of your friend, Dana Caldwell."

The high colour in Maria's cheeks drained quickly. "What? Why? Has new evidence come to light after all these years?"

Sally smiled. "Something like that. We believe her remains were found a few days ago, and we've since spoken to her husband and family, and they've confirmed that the two rings found with the corpse belonged to Dana."

Maria's head jutted forward, and her mouth gaped open for a few seconds until she recovered from the shock. "Bloody hell, I never thought this day would come. So the rings are the only way that Dana can be identified? What if someone stole her rings? What if it isn't her?"

"We're at the initial stage of our findings. The Forensic team and the pathologist are doing all they can to get the results back to us promptly."

She shook her head. "Damn. I just don't know what to say. How have Rob and her family taken the news? Jesus, don't answer that, it was a really stupid question, one that shouldn't have left my mouth."

"Not at all, an obvious question. As you can imagine, they've been hit by mixed emotions. They still have a lot of questions they need answers to, but as yet, we're unable to supply them with any."

"I can imagine. Poor things. We've all kept our fingers crossed over the years, in the hope that she would come back to us, unharmed. Now to be told this upsetting news. Well, I don't think I can put into words what I'm feeling right now. My dear friend, did she suffer?"

"Again, we won't be able to give you the answer until the pathologist and her team have assessed the crime scene and the injuries found on the corpse."

"Injuries, were there any?"

"Again, I'm not at liberty to say at this time. What I would like to get from you is your account of what happened the evening Dana went missing."

"My account? Are you going to speak to the others, too?"

"Oh yes, Abby gave us a list of people who joined you on that night out. She also told us that you were the one walking home with Dana, is that correct?"

Maria ran a hand over her pale cheeks. "I was. I've had six years full of nightmares, I can tell you. Knowing that I might have been able to save her, if only I hadn't decided to stop off… to have a wee. I've often wondered if there was someone following us that night."

"I take it you didn't see anyone or were confronted by someone on your way home?"

"No. When I paused to go to the toilet, I came out from behind the shrubs and she was gone. I searched for the next ten minutes but, well, I was a little worse for wear and gave up easily than I would have done had I been sober. I searched for her with the others, for days, but we couldn't find her. The police were useless. They accused Rob even though he was up north in Newcastle at the time of her disappearance. The officer in charge of the case was pathetic in my eyes. He didn't have a bloody clue on how to speak to any of us. Showed very little, if any, compassion."

"So I've heard. Now that we think we've preliminarily identified the remains, I'm going to go back to the office and look over the case, see if there were any leads that the officer in charge missed."

"And what about Rob? Will he be put under the microscope again? I'm sure Michael, Dana's brother, will have his say on that one."

"We've already had the pleasure of meeting him, and yes, he told us in no uncertain terms what he thought about Rob. What's your opinion on the subject? Do you believe he could have had something to do with Dana's death?"

"Bloody hell, back then I wasn't really sure what to believe. I suppose it raised my suspicions when that copper arrested him, but then he let him go without charging him. It was an unnecessary intrusion into our lives that we could have done without. We used to be all very close at the time. It ripped Rob's relationship with Dana's family apart. When he needed them the most, they took great pleasure in turning their backs on him. We didn't, his friends, although it did put a strain on our friendship, you know, to have that underlying doubt running through our minds."

"I can understand that being the case. When was the last time you saw Rob?"

"A few years back. I was there when he announced to the group that it was time for him to move on and that he and Abby were an item."

"And what type of reaction did that news get?"

"Mixed, I suppose you'd call it. I was pleased for both of them. Abby is a lovely girl, similar character to Dana, so I can see why he was attracted to her. The only stumbling block for me was the fact that Dana's body hadn't been found. That led me to believe that she had possibly run off somewhere; what if she came back and found them together, how would Dana react to that news?"

"Can you think back to around her disappearance? Did Dana ever confide in you about something that might have been possibly unnerving her?"

Her gaze drifted to the front door. "No, I don't think so. She was pretty happy in her work and her personal life. Did you ask her family?"

"Yes, they pretty much said the same thing."

"There you go then, we can't all be wrong, can we?"

"I guess so. Going back to the night it happened, how drunk would you say she was?"

"We'd all had a few drinks and the air probably hit us and sent us a bit squiffy but we definitely had our wits about us."

"When you were behind the bushes, did you hear any footsteps, anyone approach Dana or walk past the area?"

"It was so long ago now, it's hard to recall every intricate detail."

"I know, sorry to have put you in such an awkward position. Is there anything else you'd like to add?"

"I can't think of anything."

"Okay, I suppose we'll have to leave it there then. I'll give you one of my cards. Will you get in touch later if you should think of anything?"

Sally slid the card across the desk, and Maria examined it briefly, smiled and nodded.

"I will. I hope you find out what happened to our sweet friend soon. She was far too young to die."

Sally rose from her chair. Jack did the same, then he closed his notebook and put it in his pocket.

"Thanks for seeing us at such short notice."

"What else could I do? Anything to assist the police during an investigation."

Sally smiled and walked out of the building.

"She seemed all right. A bit cut up about the news, but nothing compared to the family," Jack said on the way back to the car.

"I wouldn't have expected her to have been as bad as the family. Glad to see she still cares after all these years, though."

"Are we moving on to the next one now?"

"Might as well. Who's next on the list?"

"Take your pick, three friends: Liz Baddock, Kathryn Fox and Claire Sams."

"Go in alphabetical order. Baddock first."

Sally slid behind the steering wheel, and Jack withdrew his phone from his pocket.

He put it on speaker. "Hi, is that Liz Baddock?"

"It is, who wants to know?"

"I'm DS Blackman from the Norfolk Constabulary. Would it be possible to drop by and see you?"

"What would the police want with me?"

"It's a delicate matter. Would it be convenient to visit you now? We're out and about at the moment, you see."

"If you insist. But why?"

"Like I said, it's a delicate matter, regarding an incident that took place several years ago."

She gasped and whispered, "My God, is this to do with Dana?"

"Yes. Would you mind giving me your address?"

"It's twenty-six Mallow Road in Banham."

"Ah, yes, I think I know it. Are you at home now?"

"I am. I'm off work at present."

"We should be with you in around fifteen minutes, if that's okay?"

"Whatever. See you soon."

* * *

THE HOUSE WAS in a row of terraced properties, most of which were in dire need of repair. Sally shuddered and applied the handbrake outside.

"Heck, I dread to think what we're going to encounter inside, if the outside is anything to go by."

"Let's hope it's a case of never judge a book by its cover." Jack laughed.

Sally exited the car, hoping he was right. A young woman was standing at the front window. She gave a brief wave, and the next second the front door opened, and she was there to greet them. Her dressing gown, pulled tight around her, had stains on the chest, and one of the pockets had come unstitched and was hanging loose.

Sally fixed a smile in place and showed the woman her ID. "I'm DI Sally Parker, and this is my partner, Jack Blackman. He's the one you spoke with earlier. Thanks for agreeing to see us at such short notice."

"It's okay. I'm keen to hear what you have to say about Dana. We all still miss her very much. Do you want to come in?"

"That'd be great. Thanks."

The carpet in the hallway was old-fashioned, consisting of large flowers and swirls, as well as appearing to be threadbare in several sections. Liz showed them into the first room they came to. She switched the TV off and the *Loose Women* and their live audience disappeared, leaving the room quiet.

"Take a seat. Can I get you a drink? The kettle's just boiled."

Sally waved her hand. "Thanks for the offer, but we're fine."

Liz sat in the armchair close to the gas fire that had a slight flame glowing. Sally and Jack sat next to each other on the sofa.

Liz shuffled forward to the edge of her seat and clasped her hands together. "What is this about exactly?"

"Unfortunately, we have some bad news to share."

Liz's eyes squeezed shut, and she shook her head. "No, have you found her?"

Sally sighed. "Yes, we believe so."

Liz fell quiet, and tears soon developed and dripped onto her cheeks. "Do her parents know? Last I heard, her father wasn't too well after suffering a stroke."

"Yes, we visited them earlier. Her mother, brother and sister are all aware that her body was discovered a few days ago."

"Why now? Why are you here now?"

"As you can imagine, now that a body has been found there's an urgent need for us to reopen the case. Abby gave us a list of people who Dana was out with that night. It's our intention to speak to everyone who was there, to see if they can give us any information that might help us with our enquiries."

"I see. Yes, we were out enjoying ourselves on a girls' night out; I think it was Kathryn's birthday." She paused and inhaled a few breaths, then continued, "I'm sorry. I'm off work at the moment, suffering from a bout of depression. I haven't been the same since Dana went missing, and now you're here, telling me that her body has been found. Where? What state was it in after all these years? Maybe I shouldn't ask that last question. Oh God, that poor woman. As time marched on and there was still no sign of her, some of them believed that she had run off, but I could never get my head around that idea. She loved us, why would she go off without letting us know that she was safe and well?"

"Why would a few of you think that way? Was her marriage okay?"

"Yes, as far as I knew. Rob did his best for them, worked really long hours and away from home a number of days a week for extra bonuses, to make their lives better."

"And Dana was okay with the situation?"

"Yes, she had her work and lived for her weekends when they could be together."

"Sounds like they had a firm marriage then."

"Let's just say I never had a reason to question Dana about how happy she was. That's why I struggled to believe some of the others when they said they thought she had run off. It wasn't in Dana to do that, just up and leave like that. I had a feeling something bad had happened to her. I didn't tell the others, but every night for a year, I finished work for the day and went down there, to the spot where she went missing and stayed there for a couple of hours, praying that she would come back to us."

"In all weathers?" Sally asked, amazed by the woman's dedication to her long-lost friend.

"Yes, rain or shine. Even when it was pitch-black out there at times. Is it any wonder I ended up with mental health issues? As far as any of us were concerned, she had no reason to just disappear. Some thought she'd simply had enough and walked away, but I knew deep down they were wrong. Who does that? Leaves their family and close friends without even bothering to say goodbye?"

"I have to say that scenario is more common than you'd believe."

"Really? Wow, had I realised what the likely statistics were at the time, maybe I would have reconsidered trekking down there every night."

"You're a good friend, Liz. No one can take that away from you. I'm sorry Dana's disappearance has affected you in such a devastating way."

"There was no reason for her to disappear like that. Maria should have kept a closer eye on her instead of going behind that bush to have a wee."

Sally shrugged. "Needs must, I suppose."

"I guess, but her guilt soon waned, I can tell you. Had I been in her shoes… well, it doesn't bear thinking about, knowing what state of mind I've been in since Dana left us."

"You should go easy on yourself. None of this was your fault."

"How do you know that? I mean, it wasn't, but is it right of you to just take my word for it? Is that how policing works?"

"No, a lot of the time we work off gut instinct. I can tell you've been through a rough deal since Dana was reported missing."

"I have, but this isn't about me. Where was she found? Was there any evidence discovered at the scene for you to get started on?"

"Her body was located in an abandoned house close to Thetford Forest. The scene was disturbed when someone broke into the house. Her remains were discovered in a bed upstairs, and when the man approached the bed, it fell through the ceiling. That kind of disturbance would have done untold damage to the crime scene."

"Wait, can you back up a bit? I don't understand, my head is a little fuzzy, due to the tablets the doctor put me on a few months ago. You said you found her remains. How the heck do you know it's her?"

Sally smiled. "I should have explained it properly to you. We discovered a couple of rings with the body, and the pathologist gave us a rough idea of how long she thought the person had been dead. We consulted the missing person files we had from twenty sixteen and seventeen, and four names came up. A couple of members of my team visited two families on the list, and we took the other two. When we visited Rob, he identified the rings as being Dana's."

"Ah, that makes things a lot clearer in my head now. I should ask how Rob is."

"He was upset but also relieved by the news. The same can be said of Dana's family."

"Heck. Are they still blaming Rob? I thought they were way off the mark when they refused to speak to him after she disappeared. He needed their support, and the first thing they did, after accusing him, of course, was to cast him aside. Who would do such a thing?"

"They had their reasons. I'm in two minds about it. If they felt deep down he was to blame, then maybe their reactions were justified. I don't suppose it helped when the officer in charge of the investigation chose to arrest Rob."

"Yeah, you're right. What a terrible thing to happen, to Rob, I mean. To be treated like a common criminal when you're an emotional wreck. I dread to think how something like that would have affected me."

"It was unnecessary. I've since apologised for the mishandling of the investigation, and Rob was gracious enough to accept the apology, but it should never have occurred in the first place."

"Too right. He has always had my backing, even though I lost contact with him a while back. I cut them all off really. Found it far too stressful being in touch when the main topic of conversation was Dana all the time. It wore me down in the end."

"Perhaps knowing that her body has been found and that she will soon be laid to rest will be the news you need to get you back on the road to good health."

"I hope so. I'm sick to death of taking time off work because I can't handle being around people day in, day out. I tend to have little to no patience these days and go off the handle at the flick of a switch."

"Understandable. The mind is a very complex part of our systems. I have to ask if there is anything you think we should be aware of that happened around that night."

Liz contemplated the question for several seconds and then shook her head. "I really haven't got it in me to think that far back, I'm sorry. Blame the medication. I do, frequently."

Sally smiled. "Don't worry about it. We're going to leave you to it now, unless you have any questions you want to ask?"

"I can't think of any. I'm shocked, truth be told, but also relieved. When do you think the funeral will be held? I'd like to pay my final respects to Dana, if I'm allowed."

"I'll pass that on to the family. It probably won't be for a few weeks yet."

Liz's head bowed, and she stared at her clenched hands. "I hope she didn't suffer too much."

"I don't think we'll ever know that. Try not to dwell on it too much."

"Hard not to, but I'll do my best."

Sally and Jack both stood.

"Stay there," Sally said, "We'll see ourselves out."

"If you're sure. I think this conversation has taken too much out of me. To tell you the truth, I'm not sure my legs will hold me up."

"Wishing you better health soon, Liz. Thanks again for speaking with us. Take care of yourself."

"Thank you. Please do your best for her family."

"I will, I promise."

THE NEXT STOP was the birthday girl's hairdressing establishment.

"Is Kathryn around?" Sally asked the receptionist on duty in the plush salon.

"She's just finished up with Mrs Silver, do you want to take a seat? She shouldn't be too long now."

"Thanks, we'll wait."

Sally and Jack sat in the waiting area. Sally picked up one of the hair magazines splayed on the table and flicked through it. "What do you reckon?" She showed Jack a picture of a woman with a Mohican haircut, the tuft of which had been dyed bright orange.

"Fuck, the chief would kick you out of the station within minutes of you setting foot over the threshold if you dared to show up for work like that."

Sally laughed. "As if I would. Does Donna have a favourite style?"

"Pass, ask me another."

"What the actual… don't tell me you don't take interest in your wife's appearance?"

"Umm…"

A woman with sleek black hair, wearing a tight pink uniform, appeared beside Jack.

"Saved by the interruption," he muttered.

"Hi, you wanted to see me? I'm Kathryn Fox, owner of this establishment, and you are?"

Sally discreetly showed the woman her ID. "DI Sally Parker and DS Jack Blackman. We were wondering if you had a spare minute to speak with us."

"Oh right. Have we done something wrong?"

"No, not at all. Our visit is to do with an old case we're working on."

"I see, follow me, we'll talk in my office."

The office was at the end of a long corridor. It was a lot neater than some Sally had visited lately.

"Won't you take a seat? I should have offered you a drink, sorry."

"We're fine, thanks all the same."

"Okay, I'm listening. What case are you working on?"

"The Dana Caldwell case."

The colour instantly drained from Kathryn's cheeks. "Oh shit, after all this time. Hell on earth, has something happened?"

Sally nodded. "We believe we've found Dana's body, and yes, her next of kin have been informed. Rob's girlfriend, Abby, kindly gave us a list of the people who were out with Dana the evening she went missing. We're spending the day interviewing people to see what they can remember."

Kathryn inhaled a large breath and let it seep out slowly. "It was appalling. All we did was go out and have some fun. It was my birthday, and before you ask, no, we didn't drink until we were paralytic. We were responsible drinkers, all of us."

"Although you were slightly tipsy, I gather."

"Yes, I'll give you that. But I'd say we didn't go over the top at all. The evening shouldn't have ended the way it did.

We were all beside ourselves when the news was announced the next day."

"How did you hear about it?" It was one question Sally should have asked the others.

"It was Maria. She rang each of us the next morning. Told us that Dana had just vanished into thin air. She was traumatised. It wasn't until the next day that she rang the police. That was after each and every one of us tried our best to contact Dana and failed. I was the one who urged her to make the call, and we all showed up at the station in force to report Dana missing."

"Ah, okay, that makes sense. We weren't aware of how things had panned out at the time."

"How's Rob?"

"He's bearing up. As is Dana's family. They're all aware, we shared the news with them earlier."

"They must be traumatised. I've thought about this day arriving so many times before but dismissed it as the years went by. That poor girl. I do hope she didn't suffer too much, although I fear the opposite is true. Why is it no longer safe to be a woman out at night in our society?"

"We're doing our best to combat that injustice. Every person, male and female, has a right to walk the streets at night without repercussions."

"That's the way it should be. We have equal rights nowadays."

"I agree. What we're asking Dana's family and friends is if anything untoward either happened that night or on the days prior to Dana going missing. Can you recall anything?"

Kathryn glanced at the photo on her desk—it was of a man and two children. "No, not that I can think of. It all came as a total shock to us. One minute she was there with us, having fun at my party, and the next day, she was gone, never to be seen again."

"What state was her marriage in?"

"It was okay. In my opinion, she and Rob made the perfect couple. It took him a while to move on. Abby is such a sweetheart, she fell for him heavily around the time Dana went missing. She showed him more compassion than anyone else. Don't get me wrong, she didn't go in for the kill, jump on him in his hour of need as it were, it took years for them to get together. I'm so happy for them. God, this might ruin their relationship now."

"I doubt it. Not if they've been through so much together. I hear Rob fell out with Dana's family, is that right?"

"Yeah, at the time we all thought it was really bad but we made the decision to keep out of it. It was between them, we didn't want and preferred not to take sides with either of them. All we set out to do was be there for everyone. If and when they needed us."

"That was kind of you. It must have been hard for all of Dana's friends, too, you guys. Not knowing where she was or what had happened to her that night."

"It was the pits. Her face was everywhere I looked, can you imagine that? In a salon full of mirrors. The number of times I glanced up to speak to my customers only to find they had morphed into Dana, it was such a weird and unexplainable sensation. One that ate away at me for months until the day I finally resigned myself to never seeing her again."

"I can only imagine what that must have been like for you. Some people are far more sensitive to things like that than others."

"It took a while. The others never knew how it really affected me. I believe it was the guilt playing a major part in what was going on up here." She tapped away at her temple.

"Guilt? I don't understand. What did you have to feel guilty about?"

She tipped her head back, stretched her neck out and flicked it from one side to the other. Eventually, she whispered, "We went out to celebrate my birthday. I invited everyone, and only Dana didn't get home that night. If anyone should have gone missing or died that evening, it should have been me, not her. She didn't deserve to die, it should have been me."

"No, no, no, you shouldn't think that way, Kathryn, ever. It was a coincidence, not premeditated. No one could have predicted how the night would have ended, no one."

Large tears filled her eyes and slipped onto her cheeks. "Nothing you say will ever change my mind. This feeling is deep-rooted, it's been festering, lying in the background for years, and now... now she's been found, and all those suppressed emotions that I have successfully locked away will resurface again. Life can be so cruel; why is it so unfair? Why? Why are we always surrounded by such evil, people walking through the streets with nothing but wicked thoughts running through their minds? How can we protect ourselves from people like that, with one intention in this life? I'm sorry, I'm being maudlin now."

"Don't worry, if you need to vent and let the emotions out, feel free to do just that. Have you seen a counsellor over the years?"

"No, the thought has never crossed my mind. In the main, I've coped. Blocked out, or should I say locked away my true feelings when I felt it was necessary rather than confide in the others. We're still really close these days. Let me correct that, everyone is close except for Liz. She took the news badly and has been under the doctor for a while, suffering from depression, I believe. I've tried to reach out to her several times, more so in the beginning, but she was having none of it. Made it perfectly clear that she wanted nothing more to do with us."

"Don't you find that a little strange?" Sally asked.

"At times, yes. But then I've sat back over the years and assessed the way I've coped with Dana going missing and came to the conclusion that everyone deals with loss or grief differently. No cap fits all, does it?"

"No, I suppose that's true. Might it be worth reaching out to her again, now that we believe we've discovered Dana's body?"

Kathryn shrugged and glanced over Sally's shoulder at the door. "Possibly. I'll give it a go and ring her this evening. Let's face it, it can only go one of two ways."

Sally smiled and nodded. "Thanks, I'm sure that deep down she will appreciate any effort her friends, or should I say former friends, put into contacting her right now."

"If you say so. How is she?"

"Hard to say. She was at home, still in her dressing gown when we stopped by to visit her."

"Does she still have a job or has she lost it?"

"No, she still has it."

"That's one thing, I suppose."

"I'm sure she's just waiting for one of you to reach out to her again. She's going to need the extra support now that the sad news has been shared."

"Yeah, I think we're all going to need that. Is there anything else? Only I have another customer due in soon and I need to prepare my station for her."

"No, I think we're done here now, unless there's anything else you wanted to add?"

"I can't think of anything. I'll leave it a day or so and give Emma a ring, to offer the family my condolences. I'm guessing the last thing she and her parents are going to want right now is to feel crowded, under pressure to answer everyone's calls."

"I think you're right. Thank you for being so considerate."

The three of them left the office, and Kathryn led the way back to the front door where she offered her hand for Sally to shake.

"It's good to meet you. I hope you get the results you're searching for soon."

"Thanks. After speaking with Dana's friends and family today, I can tell how much she was loved by everyone. My team and I will do our very best to find the answers that everyone is seeking to bring this case to its conclusion."

"I believe in you, Inspector. Good luck."

BACK AT THE STATION, Sally fell into the nearest chair as soon as she entered the main office. "That was a mentally exhausting day, one of the worst I've ever encountered."

"Coffee?" Lorne asked.

"Please, we've declined the last few, fearing we might get caught short between visits. How have you guys got on?"

Lorne prepared the two coffees and delivered them to Sally and Jack who had also collapsed at his desk. "I managed to pull up the case. When you mentioned that Rob had been arrested, I was kind of expecting to see Falkirk's name as the SIO."

Sally sat upright and reached for her cup. "Are you telling me he wasn't? I must confess, I thought the same."

"No, it was a DI McIverson."

Sally frowned. "Can't say I've heard of him, have you?"

Lorne shook her head. "I hadn't either until I started digging, and surprise, surprise, it turns out that he was a good friend of Falkirk's."

"Heck, not cut from the same cloth, I hope?"

"Stuart carried out some extra digging and found quite a few disciplinary notes in his record."

"Jesus, why didn't someone higher up see him and Falkirk

for what they were, bent coppers, and have the balls to nip it in the bud before things got out of hand?"

"You tell me, because I'm having a tough time working it out for myself," Lorne replied. "It leaves more than a sour taste in my mouth."

"Can you give me the file? I want to cast my eye over the statements, see if they all match what we've been told by those we've interviewed today."

"And if they don't?" Jack asked.

"Then we go back and question that person to find out why their stories differ to the events they told our colleagues at the time."

"Makes sense," Lorne said. "Do you need a hand?"

"No, it'll be quicker for me and Jack to trawl through them, if Jack is up to it, thank you, Lorne. I'll tell you what you can do for me."

"Name it."

"Do the financial checks on Rob Caldwell and Abby Goldsmith, if you would?"

"I'll get on it now."

The room fell silent. Everyone got on with the tasks they'd either been working on already or, in Lorne's case, the task she'd just been set. Jack reluctantly held out a hand for his share of the statements.

"Be thorough," Sally warned.

He raised an eyebrow and muttered, "If you don't trust me, you can always get someone else to give you a hand."

His gaze drifted over to Lorne, and Sally chuckled, witnessing the green-eyed monster raise its ugly head.

"Get on with it, that's an order."

He grumbled something indecipherable and studied the first statement. Sally suppressed the urge to tut and sigh loudly and got down to business.

Sally speed-read her pile of statements within thirty

minutes and sat back. "Nothing untoward in there. How about you, Jack?"

"Give me a chance, my brain doesn't compute as quickly as yours. I've only managed to get through two of them."

"And?"

"Nothing in there that was different to what Maria told us. Why am I not surprised?"

Sally wagged a finger. "Don't pull that one. We're doing this out of necessity. It would be negligent of us not to be thorough, we owe it to the victim and her family."

"All right, I know that. Plodding on."

"You do that. I'll be in my office. I want to ring Pauline, see if she's had a chance to examine the remains yet."

"I think you're pushing your luck there, but hey, when do you listen to anything I have to say?"

"Get on with it, Mr Grouchy."

Sally smiled at Lorne as she passed the desk. As Lorne hadn't tried to interrupt her during her journey, Sally took it as read that she had nothing to report so far regarding the financial side of things.

She sat behind her desk and crossed her fingers, hoping that Pauline would be able to give her better news.

"Pauline, hi, it's Sally Parker. Is it convenient to talk?"

"Oh, hi. You caught me at the right time. I decided to take a breather and top up my caffeine levels. What can I do for you?"

"Are you still working on the remains that were found at the house in Feltwell?"

"I am, in between other PMs as they turn up. Why?"

"I believe we've got a name for you."

"Really? I wasn't expecting you to come up with the goods so soon. Well done, you deserve a pat on the back. Crap, I hope I didn't come across as condescending then?"

"You did, but I'll let you off."

They both laughed.

"How did you find out?" Pauline asked.

"It was the photo of the rings that was the key. The husband of Dana Caldwell recognised them right away. Hey, we couldn't have done it without you giving us the lead in the first place."

"I did? How so?"

"You gave us a rough idea of TOD. My team immediately searched through the Missing Persons Database from around that time and came up with four possibilities. From then on, it was a process of elimination."

"Ah, I've got you. Okay, I'll make a note of the name on the file."

"Is it too early for you to tell me how she died?"

"Possibly, however, if you're prepared for me to go out on a limb?"

"I am. This will remain between you and me until you can give me a definite result."

"Very well. She had a fractured skull. The wound was at the back of the head. Possibly from blunt force trauma. Although I also detected a broken nose, a broken right arm and right leg as well."

"And the latter wounds couldn't have been caused by the fall through the ceiling at the house?"

"No, the wounds are definitely older."

"Interesting. So do you think she might have been tortured?" Sally asked.

"Hard to tell at this stage. It's a possibility, or she might have picked up the injuries during her abduction. Maybe she put up a fight and her attacker lashed out with such force they broke her bones."

"Yeah, I get that. She went missing after a night out with friends. It was a birthday party, but according to everyone who attended, she was perhaps a little tipsy but definitely not drunk."

"In other words, she dropped her guard. I take it she walked home."

"She did. She set off with another girl, Maria Adams. Maria was caught short and dipped behind a hedge to relieve herself. When she returned, Dana had disappeared."

"Damn. In that case, are we to presume that the two girls were being followed and someone swooped to abduct Dana when this Maria was indisposed?"

"Possibly. I can't logically think of any other reason why Dana should have gone missing."

"Have you spoken to the family? What did her husband have to say?"

"Initially, he was arrested at the time by the SIO, even though he was in Newcastle the night she disappeared."

"Hmm... you know as well as I do that doesn't account for much."

"Yeah, I'm aware of the need to keep an open mind, however, having spoken to him today, I got the impression he was telling the truth."

"Has he moved on?"

"How did I know that was going to be your next question? Yes, he has, but not until a few years had passed. He ended up with his wife's friend."

Pauline cleared her throat. "Oh, he did, did he? And by the sound of things, you don't seem to think there's anything wrong in that."

"I didn't say that. You're going to have to trust my instinct on this one."

Pauline laughed. "Ah, the old copper's gut instinct playing a part, is it?"

Sally pulled a face even though Pauline wasn't in the same

room as her. "Let's put it this way, I'm prepared to go with it for now."

"Which is your prerogative. All I'm advising is to keep an open mind until we have more details to go on."

"I will, you have my word."

"Right, was there anything else you needed? Only I've taken the final sip of my coffee and I'm eager to go back in there for round two."

"Talk soon. Enjoy."

Sally ended the call and rejoined the others. She checked in with Jack, apprehension coursing through her veins that he might snap her head off again.

"Another one gone through, and nothing out of order from what I can tell."

"Okay, I'm exhausted. I'll take the rest of the files home and go through them tonight."

Jack gave her the look. "Really? I'm sure Simon won't be pleased if you do that. I've got the final one to do, I'll stay behind and go over it."

"I can't tell you how tempting that prospect is, but on the other hand, I'd feel guilty as hell, leaving for home, knowing that you've been left behind. Give it to me, I'll glance at it while you guys turn everything off and get yourselves ready to go."

Jack didn't need telling twice. He passed her the file and switched off his computer. Sally perched on the desk closest to him and ran her finger quickly across the page. The statement belonged to Kathryn Fox, and her eyes misted as she read it. Her heart went out to the woman, who only hours earlier had confided in her that she was still riddled with guilt about her friend's disappearance.

"Are you okay?" Lorne startled her.

"Gosh, yes, I was miles away. Trying to picture what went

on that night and how the friends and family must have felt in the days afterwards."

"Yeah, it's such a tough time, when a family member has been abducted."

"Christ, yes, you should know, what with Charlie being snatched by that madman."

"Not only that, Jade, my sister, was also kidnapped by a serial killer a few years before that happened."

"What? I wasn't aware of that. What were the circumstances?"

"The deranged bastard only took Jade for a day or so in the end. I did a swap, me for her, and met him up at the services on the M6."

"Oh my, and you got out of it unscathed?"

"Sort of. The fucker set fire to the cabin he took us to. If it hadn't been for Sean Roberts and the team showing up when they did, I would have ended up as a heap of ash within minutes."

"Was Pete around at the time or had he passed away by then?"

"Yes, he was part of the team who worked out where this fucker was holding me. Thank God."

"It must have been a terrifying experience, Lorne."

"And some. However, it was nothing compared to Charlie going missing. That bastard held her for a few weeks."

"I remember you telling me. How you kept working I'll never know. But then, you've always amazed me with your tenacity and determination."

"My pig-headedness definitely came in useful and saw me through the tough ordeal."

"Hang on, wasn't that around the time you and Tom were having troubles and…?"

Lorne raised a hand to stop her. "Yes, when Jacques Arnaud passed away. It was my annus horribilis as the Queen would say, God rest her soul. Undoubtedly, the worst year of my life."

Sally threw an arm around Lorne's shoulder. "But you got through it, and so did Charlie. And look whom you ended up marrying."

Lorne smiled broadly, and her tears remained unshed. "I know. In some ways, I wouldn't have changed it for the world. Er... what am I bloody saying? I'm tired, it's been a long day, and obviously I've lost the ability to think straight."

Sally hugged her and smiled. "I knew what you meant, dear friend. It's all in the past now. Onwards and upwards, and you've definitely moved on to pastures new. Why don't we stop off and have a quick one on the way home? I'll drive, I can pick you up in the morning."

"Why not? I'm up for it."

"Hey, I hope the invitation is open to me as well," Jack said from behind them, obviously listening in on their conversation.

By now, the rest of the team had drifted off.

Sally rolled her eyes and mouthed to Lorne, "Is it okay with you?"

Lorne gave a brief nod and smiled.

"Come on then, we'll let you tag along, but the first round is on you."

"What the f...? Maybe I'll reconsider and stop off at my local instead. That way I can stagger home and pick the car up in the morning."

"I hope Donna won't mind," Sally replied.

"Tough if she does. Have a good evening, ladies."

They watched him go.

"That was your plan, wasn't it?" Lorne asked.

"Yep, he's so tight his arse squeaks a merry tune when he walks. I knew what his response would be to my suggestion.

Looks like it's just the two of us. Or we could call the boys, get them to join us?"

"Not tonight. I could do with it being just you and me, if you don't mind?"

"It's fine by me. Come on."

CHAPTER 7

When the phone rang at four in the morning, Sally thought something bad had happened to one of her parents, possibly her father. She answered it, trying to keep the panic out of her voice. "Hello, who is this?"

Sobbing rippled down the line. "It's me, Sally. Donna."

Sally bolted upright. She switched on the bedside light, and Simon stirred beside her. "Donna? My God, what's wrong?"

"I didn't know who else to turn to, it's Jack."

"What about him? Where are you, love?"

"At the hospital."

Hearing those three words, Sally shot out of bed. She carried out the rest of the conversation with her mobile on speaker while she quickly got dressed. "Which hospital?"

"Norfolk and Norwich University Hospital in the Accident and Emergency Department."

"Oh no. Why?"

By this time, Sally was almost fully dressed. All right, she hadn't had time for a wash, but that was the least of her worries with her partner in A & E.

"I'll be right there, Donna. How bad is he?"

"I don't know, they won't tell me anything, Sally."

"All right. I'll sort it when I get there. I'll be there in fifteen minutes."

"Are you sure? It's at least half an hour from your place."

"It's an emergency, I'll be using my siren. How are you?"

"Not coping very well at all. It's the not knowing that's getting to me. I know they're in there, still working on him, but… I'm so sorry to have rung you so early, I had to speak to someone, I'm going out of my mind with worry."

"You did the right thing. I'm leaving now. See you shortly."

"Drive carefully, I'd hate for you to have an accident as well."

"As well? Never mind, tell me when I get there."

Sally ended the call and swept back to the bed to kiss Simon goodbye. "Did you get the gist of that? I have to go, to be with her. Donna needs me."

"Go. I'm not going to stand in your way. Ring me when you can, and for heaven's sake, take care on the road."

"It goes without saying. Don't worry about me, I've got this. Poor Jack. I'm praying he's going to be all right. Damn, I was supposed to pick Lorne up to give her a lift into work this morning."

"Leave it with me. I'll wait until it's a reasonable hour and give her a call. Go."

"I'm gone. Thanks, Simon."

Dex ran downstairs with her.

Simon appeared at the top. "Leave him to me, you get on the road."

"Love you, both," she called out and slammed the front door closed behind her.

She pressed her key fob, and the doors clunked open. After buckling herself in, she took off, gravel flying in every direction until she eased off the accelerator. She drove through the gates and pressed her foot down. She decided there was no need to use the siren. Instead, she switched on the lights as they would power her through the lanes. She'd use the siren as and when it was needed later around the city. Her breathing was fast and furious, matching her speed.

"My God, what if he doesn't survive? No, I can't think that way. Jack, stay with us. Don't you dare leave us. Don't you dare!"

The drive was relentless. Sally felt like she was living on the edge, her nerves in tatters. She reached the hospital and managed to locate a parking space close to the entrance. The cost would be exorbitant. *Damn, I didn't bring my purse with me.* She let out a relieved sigh when she remembered she'd tucked a twenty in her glove box only the week before, in case of emergencies, not really thinking it would ever be needed. She ran through the main entrance and followed the signs to the reception area in A & E. There, she was whisked through to triage by a porter who was having a chat with the receptionist at the time. Not long after, Donna hugged her tightly.

Sally guided her to a chair and held her hands. "Have you heard anything yet?"

"No, they won't tell me a thing. All I've seen is several doctors and extra nurses going in there. What if there's something drastically wrong, Sal? What will I do without him if he doesn't survive?"

"No, you mustn't think that way, Donna. We need to remain positive at all times. Jack's a fighter, he won't give up at the first hurdle, he's not the type. Stay here, I'll see if I can get some information out of one of the nurses."

"Believe me, I've tried. Please, stay here with me." Donna clung tighter to her hands.

"All right. Let's give it another ten minutes, then I'm going to have to find out what the hell is going on."

They sat in silence. The only noise surrounding them was the swishing of curtains and the movement of trollies being pushed around by the porters. Sally put up with the situation for so long and then squeezed Donna's hands and released them.

"Let me see what I can find out."

Sally left her chair and walked towards the swing doors at the bottom of the corridor. They opened when she was a few feet away. A young male frowned and queried what she was up to.

"May I ask where you're going?"

"Are you a doctor?" *Damn, my purse isn't the only thing I forgot to pick up, I left my warrant card at home, too.*

"I am. Are you waiting to hear some news about a loved one?"

"My friend rang me. Her husband was brought in as an emergency after a traffic accident. I'm a copper, sorry, you're going to have to take my word on that one. In my haste to get here, I left my ID at home."

"It wouldn't matter anyway. As yet, there is nothing I can tell you. We're still working on him, to save his life."

Acid burned the back of Sally's throat, and her heart sank to another level. "What? Are you telling me there's a chance we might lose him?"

He gave her an intense stare and nodded. "Yes, that's a succinct possibility. Let the staff do their very best for him. All we ask you is to be patient with us."

Sally backed up a few paces. "Please, you have to save him. He's my partner in crime, I'd be lost without him by my side."

"We're not in the habit of giving up on people. Go back to your seat. We know you're here. The second we have anything to share regarding his predicament we'll come and see you. At present, our priority remains with him and trying to save his life."

"Thank you. Do your very best for us, he's one of life's good guys, he's far too young to die."

He smiled, turned on his heel and disappeared through the swing doors again. Sally stretched out her neck to try and see the team working on Jack, but the view was too brief, and the door closed swiftly behind the doctor. She returned to report back to Donna, who stood, eager to hear any news.

"Don't get too excited. They told me they're still working on him. When was he brought in?"

"I got the call at about one-thirty."

Sally did the maths in her head and came to the conclusion that things were far worse than she had initially predicted they were going to be. "We need to think positive. They're all in there, doing their very best for us, Donna. For him."

"But the longer it goes on… well, what does that mean? I was told he had to be cut out of the car. It took them a while to get him out. What if… he's got brain damage? What if he loses a limb? How will we cope?"

"Hush now. Let's keep a clear head and not get bogged down with a lot of what-ifs. They're working on him, that's got to be a good thing, Donna. They haven't given up on him just yet, and neither should we."

"I have no intention of doing that but… I'd like to know what lies ahead of us so I can start making plans."

Sally reached for Donna's hands and encouraged her to sit. "Come now, you're thinking too far ahead of yourself. Let's take this one step at a time. You're not alone, love, don't ever think you are. We'll get through this together. Jack will pull through this, you need to have faith in him. We both know how damn stubborn he can be."

Donna released her hand from Sally's grasp and covered

her face. "I don't know. Why did he have to stop off at the pub? He should have been aware of the dangers after losing his dad in an accident a few months ago. Why didn't he take that into consideration? Selfish bastard. He's never thinking of me and the kids."

"No, no, no, Donna, that simply isn't true. He talks about you guys constantly, day in and day out, I won't have you believing otherwise."

Donna dropped her hands and stared at her through sore eyes. "He does? We love him so much. We've all been through the mire these last few years, what with dealing with a teenage pregnancy in the house."

"And you've all done an amazing job, coming through it all, relatively unscathed I might add. Just like you'll get through this. Neither of us knows what lies ahead, but he wouldn't want us to give up on him, now would he?"

"You're right. I'm not, not really. I suppose all I'm trying to be is practical."

"While that's admirable, I think you're not doing yourself any favours thinking that way until you've received further news about his injuries and the expected recovery time. Hang in there. Let's take every hour as it comes for now, agreed?"

Donna sighed, and her gaze drifted down the corridor to the swing doors at the bottom. "If you insist. Come on, guys, bring us some news."

"Where are the kids?"

"At home, tucked up in bed still. I snuck out of the house, didn't see the sense in waking them up and making their lives a misery at that time of the morning."

"See, I'm always telling Jack what a wise lady you are."

She smiled through her tears. "I have my moments. Just because I'm married and have devoted my life to bringing up the kids and looking after my husband, it doesn't mean my brain has turned to mush over the years."

"People who disrespect mothers like that should be shot, right?"

"Absolutely."

The doors swung open, and a different man in a blue uniform walked up the corridor towards them. He paused to speak to one of the porters passing by and then continued on his journey. He came to a halt in front of Donna and Sally.

"Hi, is it Mrs Blackman?"

Sally pointed at Donna. "What news do you have about Jack? I'm DI Sally Parker, Jack's my partner in the force."

"Ah, I see. I wasn't aware he was a police officer, not that it would have made any difference to the way he's been treated."

"How is he, Doc?" Sally asked, cutting to the chase.

"I believe in being honest with families. I can't lie, we've had a struggle keeping him with us."

"What? Is he conscious?" Donna asked.

"No, and he's not likely to be for a while. We've made the decision to put him into an induced coma for now. This will allow his body to heal quicker."

"What's wrong with him?" Sally asked when Donna neglected to.

"What isn't wrong with him would be easier to list. I'm jesting, sorry if you thought that was in poor taste. He's got several broken ribs, a punctured lung. He has a large wound in his chest that we're going to need to repair in the operating theatre. A shard of metal missed his heart by inches. He has a bad head injury; in all honesty, that's what we're more concerned about. We'll be sending him for an MRI scan and then on to theatre soon. Did I mention both his legs are broken from the knee down?"

Sally shook her head. "Oh heck. He's lucky to be still with us, isn't he?"

"He is. I have to tell you, that's mainly down to our efforts in triage."

"We can't thank you enough. Are you prepared to put your neck on the line and tell us what the prognosis is likely to be?"

"I'm not, it's more than I dare do at this stage. All I can tell you is that he's a fighter and it will be his sheer determination that gets him through this."

Sally grasped Donna's hands. "See, we both know that's the truth, don't we, Donna?"

"Yes. If anyone can do it, Jack can. Is it possible for us to see him?"

The doctor paused, and his gaze flitted between them. "I'm willing to forgo the protocol for now and will allow you to spend a few minutes with him. But be warned, I'm not one for sugar-coating the truth, it's not pretty in there."

"It doesn't matter, we need to see him," Sally replied. Her stomach cramped up at the thought of Jack lying there in a helpless state. She needed to keep it together, no matter how tough things got in there, for Donna's sake.

The doctor led the way. The walk was one of the longest and most angst-ridden Sally had ever taken in her life. Donna held her hand, and they linked arms on the torturous journey into the unknown. The doctor opened the familiar swing doors and crossed the room full of life-saving equipment to Jack's bed.

The second she laid eyes on him, Sally struggled to hold back the tears, but she knew she had to, for Donna's sake as well as her own. Donna faltered beside her, her legs appearing to weaken slightly. Sally held her arm firmly in case she passed out.

"Are you all right, Mrs Blackman?" the doctor asked.

"No, I don't think I'll ever be the same again. Look at the state of him. He has no right to be still here with us. Look at the injuries he's sustained."

"Try to look beyond that, Donna. He's here with us, that's all that matters."

"I know, but at what cost? The injuries he sustained in the army during his days on patrol are nothing compared to what he's dealing with now. I don't think he's got it in him to get through this." Her voice trailed off, and she shuddered.

"Nonsense. You heard the doctor, he's a born fighter." Sally stared at all the tubes puncturing her partner's body, and tears welled up again. She shook her head, trying to dislodge them. Her gaze drifted to the monitor. She watched the line spike and drop several times, her heart lurching with every peak.

"Okay, ladies. The porter is ready to take him down to surgery now. I said it would be a brief visit."

"We appreciate you allowing us to spend this time with him," Donna whispered.

"How long is the surgery likely to take?" Sally plucked up the courage to ask.

"I have no way of knowing, it's not my field of expertise, I'm sorry. Can you go back to the waiting area? I'll make sure the staff keep you informed as soon as they hear any news."

"Thank you, Doctor. We'll be fine, we don't want to impose on you further. We'll wait to hear from you."

Donna stepped closer to the bed and ran a hand around her husband's bloody face. "I love you, Jack Blackman. Don't you dare give up on us, not now you've come this far."

Sally tugged her out of the way, the porter eager to get on with his duties. Donna held it together long enough for them to return to the seating area, and then the tsunami of emotions arrived. Choked, all Sally could do was cradle her friend in her arms.

"There, there, everything will turn out for the best, I promise."

"Will it, though, Sal? After seeing the state of him in there, I'm not so sure."

Sally faced her, clutched both of her arms and held them firmly. "What did I tell you before? You, *we*, need to remain positive."

Donna nodded, and the tears flowed faster. They continued to comfort each other for the next few hours until they heard the surgery had gone well and that Jack was on his way to get a scan.

"What then? Will he be transferred to a ward? Will we be able to sit with him?" Donna asked the nurse who had delivered the news.

The nurse smiled and nodded. "I'll get someone to fetch you once he's been settled on the ward."

"Thanks," Sally replied.

The nurse left, and Donna reached out to Sally for a hug.

She obliged and checked her watch at the same time. It was coming up to seven. They continued to sit there, waiting for further news. At seven-thirty, they received the go-ahead to visit Jack who was on his way up to the men's ward. She hadn't got far when someone called out Sally's name. She turned to find a worried-looking Lorne standing there.

"My God, what are you doing here?" Sally asked. She walked into Lorne's outstretched arms.

"I woke up at five and found it hard to shift the fear of dread running through me. I left it until six-thirty and decided to check if everything was all right at the house. Simon was in the garden with Dex, he filled me in about what had happened. I got Tony out of bed, he drove me here. I told him not to wait and that I'd get a lift back with you. Never mind all of that, how's Jack?"

"I'm so pleased to see you. I'm not sure if you know Donna or not? This is Jack's wife."

"We've met in passing," Lorne replied. "How's he doing, do you know?"

"We're just on our way up to see him. The doctor told us earlier that Jack's a fighter. He also added that he's going to need to be, too, with the injuries he's sustained."

Lorne shook her head, and the tears surfaced. "How did it happen?"

"Apparently a lorry failed to stop at the junction. Jack had been at the pub. I'm guessing his reactions weren't at their best due to the alcohol, and one thing led to another and he ended up being cut out of his vehicle."

"And his injuries?" Lorne asked.

They turned a corner in the corridor, and Sally bumped into a young woman. "Maria? What are you doing here?"

Maria Adams's cheeks flushed. She held up two tightly bound fingers. "Oh, hi. I… umm… I got attacked, and the bastard broke two of my fingers, at least, that's what I thought at the time. I've since found out that they're badly bruised. They should heal within a few days."

"You were attacked? Where?" Sally was in two minds whether to continue the conversation or to carry on with her relocation to the men's ward. She glanced at Lorne whose brow was furrowed. "Sorry, this is one of Dana Caldwell's friends. She was the one who reported her missing."

"Oh, right. Where were you attacked?" Lorne asked, her voice full of sympathy.

"On my way home last night. I didn't bother coming to the hospital right away, didn't think it warranted it, but the pain got worse during the night. I finally got myself up and dressed and came down here at six this morning."

"Always better to get these things checked out," Sally said. "Do you know who attacked you?"

"No. But they told me to keep my mouth shut about Dana, so I thought it must have something to do with her murder. Do you think I'm in danger? Will this person come back and have another go at me?" Her voice shook with fear.

"I'm sorry. I hate to run off like this, but we've got an emergency of our own to attend to. Can you drop by the station later and give us a statement?" Sally asked, aware of the anxiety building in Donna beside her.

"Oh, I see. Yes, I suppose I can. What time shall I drop by?"

"After lunch, at around two if that's convenient? We might be here a while this morning."

"I hope your friend isn't too bad. I'll see you later." Maria waved and went on her way.

"You could have spoken to her longer," Donna said as they set off on their journey once more. "It's not like we're in a rush."

Sally raised an eyebrow. "Aren't we? You've been, we've both been here for hours, and apart from seeing him for a few minutes… well, I'm eager to see how he got on with his surgery, aren't you?"

Donna smiled. "Yes, you're right as usual, Sally. Silly of me not to think about that."

The three of them continued walking through the silent hospital corridors until they reached a busier wing. The men's ward was the first one they came to. They used the antibacterial gel and they all put on a mask.

"Should I stay out here?" Lorne asked. "I feel like I'm intruding."

"I don't mind you coming in with us, Lorne, if the nurses will allow it," Donna assured her.

"Thanks, Donna. Don't worry if they stick to the 'only two to a bed rule', I can wait out here."

"Let's see what they have to say," Sally suggested. "Shall I lead the way?"

Donna nodded and wrung her hands together nervously. "Yes, you might have more clout than me with the nurses."

Sally and Lorne both reached out and grabbed Donna's hands.

"You'll be fine, we'll be with you every step of the way," Sally said.

"I'm ready. Let's go."

Sally pushed open the door and entered the ward. The nurses' station was a few feet away. Two nurses were in a deep discussion about one of the patients. Sally waited for them to finish talking and then announced their arrival.

"Ah, yes. Jack Blackman. We only allow two people to see our patients per visit, but we're willing to make an exception this time, as he's a policeman. Please don't make a habit of it, though, as it could get us into hot water with the other patients."

"Don't worry, this will be a one-off, and thank you," Sally replied, her grateful smile hidden behind the mask.

"How is he?" Donna asked, trepidation filling her tone.

The older of the two nurses moved from behind the desk to join them and led the way up the ward. "The surgery went well. As far as the scan results go, we won't have those back until the doctor has had a chance to assess them. I want to assure you, he's in safe hands." She came to a stop outside a screened-off bed. She pulled the curtain back to reveal an unconscious Jack. "We always advise talking to the patient. Hearing a recognisable voice is what aids their recovery."

"Blimey, I better let you do all the talking then, Donna, he might refuse to come around if I start."

The nurse inclined her head. "Sorry, am I missing something here?"

Sally smiled and filled her in. "I'm his boss, and this is a work colleague of Jack's."

"Ah, yes, I get it now. I'm sure I don't have to tell you how to hold a conversation, but most people in this situation tend to dry up. I suggest you talk about things that are important to him, perhaps his family, children if you have any. Or hobbies he might have, like football, racing, cars, anything along those lines. Past holidays, possible adventures he's had over the years, which are not work related."

"Between us, I'm sure we can come up with a number of different topics to cover," Sally said.

"I'll get you another chair and leave the curtain drawn to give you some privacy. If I can ask you to keep the noise down, we've got some patients in need of rest on this ward."

"It goes without saying," Donna said. She moved alongside the bed and sat in the seat next to Jack's head. She held out a hand and rested it on top of her husband's. After a few seconds, she leaned forward and kissed Jack on the cheek and whispered something in his ear.

Sally watched the monitor beside her partner for any kind of reaction. There wasn't one.

Lorne took the extra chair from the nurse and placed it at the foot of the bed next to Sally's. Sally could tell how taken aback Lorne was by Jack's appearance. She squeezed Lorne's hand, reassuring her that everything was going to be all right. Lorne smiled in return. They both sat there, listening to Donna recollect old stories relating to what the pair of them had got up to in their youth. Some of those stories consisted of Jack's time in the army. He'd enjoyed his enrolment and had been saddened to leave it but had needed to due to the injuries he had sustained whilst on duty.

Half an hour later, Sally decided it was time for her and Lorne to leave. She couldn't tell if Donna was relieved or even more apprehensive to be left alone with Jack by the change of emotions in her features.

Donna stood and hugged them both and whispered, "I can't thank you enough for being here with me, with us."

"I'd like to say the pleasure was all ours, but that would be wrong in the circumstances. We're family, Donna," Sally replied. "Don't ever forget that. Reach out to us if you need to talk. Don't take this burden on yourself. Ring me day or night, you've got my number."

"Thanks, Sally. I have it in my phone. Will it be all right if I give you a call tonight?"

"I'd be upset if you didn't. Will the kids be okay? Do you want me to drop round there and make sure?"

"Yes, they're old enough to fend for themselves. I'll give them a ring in an hour or so."

"Again, if they need anything, don't hesitate to get in touch with me, I'll do my best to be there for all of you."

"What would we do without you?"

Sally hugged her again. "He's like a brother to me. We need to have faith that he's going to get better, love."

"I'll get there, eventually. Thanks for coming, both of you, it means the world to me to know that you're behind us."

"Always," Sally replied. "Speak to you later. If he wakes up, tell him he's expected back to work within a few days."

Donna's pained expression gave way to a smile. "I'll make sure he understands the urgency."

"And, you need to take care of yourself, too. That includes eating and drinking regularly."

"The truth is, I couldn't stomach anything right now. But I promise I'll look after myself when the need arises."

They shared a group hug, and Sally reluctantly left the ward with Lorne.

"Am I doing the right thing? Deserting him like this?"

Lorne flung an arm around her shoulder. "You're far from

deserting him. I have to ask the question, if Jack is that bad, why isn't he in the ICU?"

Sally mulled over her question for a second as they stripped off their masks and placed them into the bin. "Maybe they didn't have room in ICU. Should I go back and ask?"

"No, they obviously know what they're doing. I'm sure it'll be fine. Forget I mentioned it. I know you, you'll let things fester otherwise."

"Let's get to the station. Can't believe how long the day has been so far. Thanks again for coming, Lorne."

"I'll do anything to get a lift into work. Don't forget I left my car at the station last night on the understanding that you would give me a ride in this morning."

Sally tutted and rolled her eyes. "Jesus, the lengths some people will go to astounds me."

They both laughed.

CHAPTER 8

The team were all eager to hear the news about Jack. Shocked faces gave way to relieved smiles once Sally had finished filling them in about his status. "So, it's back to work for us all. We're one man down, that means we're all going to have to work that much harder to achieve the results we're after. Needless to say that Lorne will be stepping up to take Jack's place alongside me. I'll leave Lorne to fill you in about what happened at the hospital with one of the witnesses on the case, while I go and see the DCI. He'll string me up if I fail to keep him in the loop."

She swept out of the office and up the corridor to DCI Green's office. Lyn, his PA, glanced up and smiled. "Hello, Inspector. Is he expecting you this morning?"

"Sorry to drop in unannounced, Lyn, it's an urgent matter that just can't wait."

"I'll see what I can do for you. Take a seat."

"I'd rather stand, if it's all the same. I've been sat around at the hospital for hours."

Lyn rose from her seat and knocked on her boss's door.

She stuck her head into the room and said, "Inspector Parker is here to see you, sir."

"Did I miss an appointment on my calendar?"

"No, sir. It's an urgent matter. Shall I show her in?"

"Yes, okay. I've got a call coming in at ten, haven't I?"

"You have indeed."

"Very well, remind me at five minutes to, if you will?"

"I'll do that, sir." Lyn dipped back into the outer office and beckoned Sally. "DCI Green will see you now, Inspector."

Sally swept past her. "I shouldn't be too long."

"Coffee?"

"I'd never say no, thanks, Lyn."

"I'll bring it in for you, he's due one anyway."

Sally knocked on the door out of habit before she entered. "Hello, sir. Thank you for seeing me at short notice."

"Take a seat. What's this concerning, Sally?" He placed his pen on the desk and gave her his full attention.

"I have bad news to share. I've spent half the night at the hospital with Jack Blackman's wife."

His head tilted to the left. "Why? Is everything okay?"

"Jack was involved in a serious accident last night. His car collided with a lorry, shall we say? He had to be cut from the wreckage."

"Heck. How is he?"

"In a serious way. Lots of bad injuries, including a punctured lung. By the sounds of it, we almost lost him a few times during the night before the doctors were able to stabilise him."

"Hellfire. What can I do to help? Is there anyone I can call to make sure he's treated well in hospital? I'm not sure how these things work, Inspector."

"No, I believe he's in safe hands, sir. His wife is with him. Lorne and I both showed up at the hospital to lend our support. We're keeping everything crossed that he pulls through this."

"I will, too. My goodness, this has come as a complete and utter shock to me. How are you bearing up? I know how close you guys are."

"As long as I keep going, I'll be fine. It's when I stop and have time to think that it will probably hit me."

The door opened, and Lyn brought two cups of coffee in, set them on the desk and left again.

"Promise me you'll look after yourself, Sally?"

She smiled. "Funny, that's the last thing I said to his wife, Donna, before I left the hospital."

"Great minds," he said, a glimmer of a smile appearing on his tanned face. "Let me know if I can be of assistance with the case you're working on. How's that going? I take it Lorne will step up and temporarily fill Jack's shoes again?"

"Yes, already actioned it, sir. With regards to the case, we're getting there. Yesterday, Jack and I did the rounds, questioned all the witnesses who were out with the victim the night she went missing. I have to say, we've been disappointed by the results so far. However, a witness showed up at the hospital, she'd been attacked by someone, and the victim's name came up during the assault."

"Really? That sounds odd after all these years, doesn't it?"

"My sentiments exactly. I've asked her to come in this afternoon to make a statement. We'll see what she has to say about the attack then. I was too concerned about Jack to deal with her back at the hospital."

"That's totally understandable. What's your instinct telling you about this one? Have you stumbled across the killer yet?"

Sally took a sip from her coffee and shook her head. "Nothing is really steering me in any such direction, sir."

"And the husband? What are your feelings about him? Could he have killed the victim?"

"I don't think so. He was arrested at the time but he had a cast-iron alibi when his wife went missing. He was away at a conference all week up in Newcastle."

"Do you think it was a random kidnapping which led to her being murdered then?"

"Again, until we dig a little deeper, there's no telling what we'll be confronted with, sir. I can assure you, we're going to give it our all."

"I wasn't doubting your abilities, Sally. Look, I repeat, if you need my assistance, don't hesitate to ask. I can clear my desk within minutes."

"That's very kind, sir. If we think we're not getting anywhere, I'll be sure to come knocking on your door."

"Good. Now, you're going to have to excuse me, I have an important meeting with the super to get ready for. It can go either way, as you can imagine."

Sally stood and collected her cup. "Good luck with it, sir."

"Listen, send Jack's wife my regards. Tell her if she needs anything to reach out, either through you or you can give her my direct number, if that will help."

"Thanks, sir. She'll appreciate that. I've already told her how much he means to us all."

"Glad to hear it. Keep me updated with the case, and Jack's progress, if you will."

"You've got it. Thanks, sir." Sally left the room and paused to empty her cup before she handed it to Lyn. "It was truly appreciated, thanks, Lyn. Sorry to disrupt your morning."

"You haven't, you mustn't think like that, Inspector. I hope everything is all right?"

"Not really. My partner is laid up in hospital, fighting for his life."

"God, I had no idea. I'm so sorry to hear that, Inspector. I hope he pulls through."

Sally smiled. "So do I." She left the office and drifted back up the corridor to join the rest of the team. "How's it going?"

Lorne offered to get her a coffee.

"I've just had one."

"Okay. I was going over what you and Jack came up with yesterday and noted a name you'd highlighted with no statement attached."

"Am I supposed to know what you mean by that, Lorne? Bearing in mind my head is in a mess."

"Sorry, I should have made it clearer. Claire Sams. She's listed, but you didn't visit her. Can I ask why?"

"Damn, yes. It turns out she works in the admin department at the station. We had plans to question her yesterday afternoon when we got back, but one thing led to another, and it kind of slipped my mind. Can you give her a call? Rather than going to her, ask her if she'll nip up and have a word with us here."

"I can do that. Interesting that she should work for the police."

"Is it? I didn't really think anything of it at the time. I'll be in my office, knee-deep in post. Let me know how you get on."

She was glad to see the post was minimal this morning, she could do with an easy day on that front.

Lorne knocked on the door and entered the room a few minutes later. "She's popping up to see us during her morning break which is in ten minutes."

"Great. It'll be good to tie everything up this morning. Don't forget we've got Maria Adams coming in to see us at two."

"I hadn't. How are you holding up? I promise not to

bombard you with coffee and sympathy, I just want you to know that I'm around if you need a shoulder to cry on."

"Thanks. As long as the work keeps flowing my way, I'll be fine. That doesn't mean to say that Jack isn't constantly on my mind. Shit, I'd better ring Simon, let him know what's happening."

"I'll leave you to it. Want me to give you a shout when Claire arrives?"

"Yeah, I shouldn't be on the phone too long." She picked up her mobile and rang Simon's number.

"Hello, is this important, Sally?" he sounded off with her.

"Pardon me for breathing. I was going to give you an update on what's going on with Jack. What's eating you?"

"Damn. Sorry. Tony and I have just arrived at a house that was due to go on the market today, and it's been trashed by vandals."

"Oh no, that's dreadful. Is it really bad?"

"Bad enough. Everything is going to have to be ripped out again, and we're going to need to start over from scratch."

"Bloody hell. Won't the insurance cover it?"

"Probably, but it's still going to put our schedule behind. Never mind, that's our problem. Sorry for having a pop at you. How's Jack?"

"In a bad way. Punctured lung, a couple of broken legs to name only a few of his injuries."

"Poor bloke. That's tough. When can he come home?" he asked, still sounding distracted.

"I wish I knew. They've put him in an induced coma. It doesn't look good, Simon."

"I'm sorry to hear that, love. You need to think positively about his chances. He's a fighter. If anyone can get through this, it's Jack."

"Yeah, I said the same to Donna earlier. What will you do about the damage?"

"Tony's going around the house now, taking dozens of photos for the insurance people. We'll get the claim in today and get the ball rolling with making the place more secure, changing the locks et cetera. Damn, Sally, you should see this place. It's galling to see it in such a state. I'll send you a few shots. Hang on, bear with me, you know I'm not the best where technology is concerned."

Sally tapped her fingers on the desk and waited for her phone to notify her that the images had arrived. "Hang on, they're here. Let me flip through them, stay on the line." She opened the first image and gasped. "Bloody hell, this is criminal." The photos were of the newly fitted kitchen they'd only put in a few weeks earlier. Every cupboard and work surface had been wrecked by what would appear to have been a sledgehammer. She flicked through the rest of the photos and then spoke to Simon with tears of frustration misting her vision. "Jesus, that's utterly diabolical. Have you informed the police?"

"Yes, sorry. I should have said. They're going to send someone around, when they have the time."

"Leave it with me. I'll have a word with the desk sergeant after we've finished. I'll make sure someone is with you within the hour. You should have called me, sweetheart. I could have actioned it sooner."

"To be honest, we've only been here thirty minutes. It's taken me a while to calm down and stop swearing. First port of call was the insurance people. Hey, and I figured you'd have enough on your plate, worrying about Jack."

"I know. I'm sorry this has happened to you. Is it going to cost much to put right?"

"How long is a piece of string? They've been thorough, ripped out the plumbing. We've got leaks galore to deal with up in the bathroom. Luckily, we had a plumber on site, a couple of doors away, so he's on the case already."

"Okay, I'm going to do what I can for you at this end. Don't let this get you down, love."

"I'm trying not to. See you later."

"I love you. Keep that chin high."

"Love you, too."

She hung up, and Lorne entered the room.

"Sorry to interrupt, hey, what's up?"

Sally threw her pen across the room and angled her phone in Lorne's direction. "The house that was due to go to market this week has been vandalised."

"Fuck. That's a lot of damage to deal with."

"You're not kidding. I'm about to ring the desk sergeant, get him to send a couple of our boys over there. Simon has been given the brush-off this morning by our lot."

"Ouch! I've heard on the grapevine there have been a spate of these types of cases lately. Maybe they're inundated down there. Claire is here, do you want me to deal with her? Bearing in mind she's on her break."

"Shit! Yes. I'll join you in a few minutes, once I've contacted the front desk."

"Okay. Good luck."

Sally inhaled a few deep breaths and made the call. "Pat, it's Sally Parker. I need to ask you a huge favour."

"Name it, I'll do anything for my favourite inspector."

Sally grinned. "You're a gem. I hope I'm not pushing the boundaries here."

"I won't know until you tell me, will I?"

"My husband reported that one of the houses he's been renovating has been vandalised and was told someone would attend when they had the time. Is there any chance you can up the priority on that for me?"

"Let me see if I can find the call." Paper rustled, and then he came back on the line. "Here it is. I'll get it actioned right away. I had no idea it was Simon's place. He should have mentioned it when he placed the call."

"He didn't like to. Thanks, Pat. I owe you one. I've heard there's a spate of these going on at the moment. Are you any closer to finding out who's causing all this damage?"

"Not yet. I don't suppose your husband has installed any cameras at the house, has he?"

"I'm not sure. I can check."

"If he hasn't, my advice would be to change that in the future. Obviously, it would need to be a discreet one, placed here and there, nothing that will stand out."

"I'll make sure that happens. Thanks, Pat."

"Anytime, ma'am, you know that."

Sally hung up and joined Lorne in the outer office. Claire Sams was in her mid-thirties, and her long, shiny hair was her stand-out feature. Sally drew up a chair next to Lorne.

She extended her hand towards Claire. "I've seen you around, Claire. Sorry to have to call you in like this, and I also want to apologise for not getting around to interviewing you sooner. Time has been our greatest enemy so far."

"It's okay. I was sorry to hear about your partner, ma'am. I've heard on the grapevine that he's fighting for his life. I'll be sure to say a silent prayer for him tonight."

"Thank you. We're trying to do all we can to remain positive. Anyway, that's by the by. How have you got on?" Her question was directed at Lorne.

"Claire was just telling me about an ex-boyfriend of Dana's who we might be interested in seeking out."

"Oh, tell me more."

Claire sighed and ran a finger along the edge of her jumper. "Scott Davis. At the time Dana went out with him, he had a few personal issues, but that's not why I mentioned him."

"Oh, why then?"

"Because he was besotted with Dana when they were both in their teens."

"Was he now? In this area?"

"Yes, Dana went to school just up the road from here. We all did. He used to follow us everywhere. His main aim was to become part of our gang."

Sally frowned. "Would that have been an all-female gang?"

"Mostly, until our later years when a couple of us hooked up with fellas and they tagged along with us."

"And what happened? Did he take the hint that Dana wasn't interested come the end?"

"We were in sixth form, she was seventeen and he was nineteen. One day, in the middle of winter, we were on our way out of the girls' changing rooms to the field at the back of the school for a game of rounders. He cornered us, or should I say her, in the corridor. His constant attention-seeking had gone on for months and, well, Dana eventually snapped. She told him in no uncertain terms where to go. He shocked us all by grabbing her around the throat and pinning her to the wall."

"That must have been terrifying for you all," Sally said. "What happened next?"

"Thankfully, a male teacher heard us all screaming at him to let her go and dealt with the situation. He was then escorted off the premises and kicked out of school."

"Did he go quietly? Sorry, I mean did he just accept his fate for what it was or did he cause more trouble for Dana, you know, out of school?"

"He hung around for a while, but then her brother, Michael, got wind of what he was up to, and he and a couple of his friends went around there and had it out with him."

"And did that do the trick?"

"We thought so at the time until we saw him in town on a

night out. He was alone in the pub we went to. We were celebrating my eighteenth birthday, and he came over to wish me a happy birthday. Dana visibly shrank away from him. He refused to take no for an answer when we told him to bugger off. I couldn't stand all the tension and had a word with the manager who got the bouncer to kick him out."

"Don't tell me, he was outside, waiting in the bushes or something like that."

"No, he left, thank God. We were dreading leaving the pub that night. We stayed way after last drinks were served, most of us too frightened to go outside in case he was lingering and started causing shit again."

"And after that? Were there any other problems with him?"

"No, maybe a few minor incidents, but nothing major. Mind you, by this time, Dana had hooked up with Rob, so perhaps that put a stop to Scott's shenanigans."

"Can you think back to the night Dana went missing? Do you remember seeing him at any of the pubs or the nightclub you visited?"

She shook her head. "That's asking a lot. I have to say no, but it wouldn't be a confident answer."

Sally smiled. "Don't worry about it. And it's Scott Davis? I don't suppose you knew his address back in the day, did you?"

"He lived close to Greenaway School, I believe. But I couldn't tell you where exactly. I tried to ignore him when I could, lacked interest in him because all he did was give me the creeps."

"Odd question coming up: did he show up at Dana and Rob's wedding?"

"Gosh, now you're testing me. I don't think so. I guess he must have got over her once she started going out with Rob then, right?"

"Possibly. We'll see if we can track him down and have a chat with him."

"I would definitely note him down as a person of interest if I were leading the investigation." Her head dropped, and the finger that had been playing with her jumper shifted to circle the rim of her mug. "I was devastated to hear that she had been found. I can't imagine the pain and suffering she must have experienced before her death. Fancy the person who killed her leaving her body lying around to rot and not giving her a proper burial."

"The sign of a crazy person, perhaps?" Sally said, more to herself than to Lorne and Claire.

"You've got that right," Claire responded. "She was one of the nicest people I have ever known. One of my dearest friends. I know that's probably the first thing people say about their friends after their passing but, believe me, it's true in Dana's case."

"By what everyone has said about her, we know that's the truth."

Claire glanced up at the clock on the wall and tutted. "I'm sorry to cut this short but I have to get back to work now. My boss is a stickler for good time-keeping, and I haven't let her down yet."

"Go. You've been more than helpful. Please consider what we've asked you during this interview, and if anything else should come to mind, will you ring me?" Sally slid a card across the desk to Claire.

"Of course. My mind has probably blocked out a lot of the events from that night, trying not to dwell on the fact that it was the last time any of us saw Dana. Do you know when the funeral is likely to be?"

"I don't. Are you still in touch with the family?"

"Yes, sort of. We go out with Emma now and then but, as

a group, we decided that we wouldn't mention Dana's name again, in case it upset her too much talking about her."

"I can understand your logic there. Thanks for all the information you've given us. We're going to do our best to track Davis down. It should be easy enough, providing he hasn't moved out of the area."

"Good luck. Please, do your best for Emma and her family, they need to know the truth behind Dana's disappearance and how she ended up… dead."

"You have my word. We're old hands at this type of thing now."

Lorne walked Claire to the door and then returned to sit next to Sally. "How did you get on with the vandalism?"

"Pat's moving it up his list of priorities as a favour to me. I feel bad asking him to do it, but you know how much effort has gone into that place. He suggested putting discreet cameras in all the houses being renovated."

"Wow, that could get costly."

"What's the alternative? We need to catch these bastards in the act. Moving on, let's get cracking with what Claire has told us."

"How likely do you think it will be for him to be involved?"

Sally shrugged. "I won't know until I've had a chat with him. He sounds a right moron to me, unpredictable enough to do some real damage, if pushed."

"That's the key, isn't it? How far his type needs to go before something drastic happens? I'll make a start." Lorne tapped Scott's full name into the computer and nodded. "Well, that was easy enough. Whoa, he's a pharmacist now."

"Is he really? Maybe he saw the error of his ways and set out to turn his life around," Sally suggested. "Do you have an address for him?"

"Yep. I've got his home address and where he works on the system."

"Great news. We'll try his workplace first, seems logical for this time of day. Are you ready to head out now?"

Lorne bared her teeth in a soppy grin. "I might have to make a pit stop first. Too many cups of coffee to my name today."

"I'll come and hold your hand."

They both laughed. Lorne headed to the loo first while Sally brought the rest of the team up to date.

"Joanna, can you jump ahead for us? Search for Scott Davis's financial details and run any necessary background checks on him ASAP. Get back to us with the information if anything interesting shows up. See you later. The rest of you, carry on digging."

Sally walked into the ladies' to find Lorne running a finger over the lines on her face and studying her greying hair.

"You're as young as the man you feel," Sally said and swept into one of the cubicles.

"I'm up shit creek then, Tony is older than me."

"Damn, I forgot that. You're fine, you worry too much. I bet you still feel twenty-five inside, don't you?" She flushed the toilet, opened the door and washed her hands next to Lorne.

"I do. Although you want to hear the amount of creaks and groans my body experiences when I get out of bed every morning."

Sally laughed. "Something to look forward to in my old age."

Lorne swiped her upper arm. "Cheeky mare. I'm not over the hill just yet."

"Hey, it's not me complaining about the amount of grey

hairs on your head and the creases on your face. Come on, let's get this show on the road. Is the pharmacy far?"

"I reckon it's at least twenty minutes."

"The sooner we tackle the issue, the less time there is for it to fester, a once very wise woman told me. I forget her name now, it was some bird working in the Big Smoke at the time."

"I think I know the wench. I wonder what happened to her."

"Silly bitch retired early to the country. Last I heard she had rejoined the force for I think about the fourth time. She's like the proverbial boomerang, always coming back."

"Hey, I've just remembered, we can't be gone too long, we've got Maria Adams coming in at two."

Sally punched her thigh. "Damn, I'll admit, it had slipped my mind."

They tore down the stairs and out to Sally's car.

"Do you want me to drive?" Lorne asked.

"Lacking confidence in my driving skills? I know I asked you to stand in for Jack while he's indisposed, but that's taking the piss, partner."

Lorne shook her head. "I was offering to give you a break. You've been up hours, far longer than me. I won't bother next time."

"I'm fine. The day I stop plodding on through adversity is the day they cremate me. You hear me, I don't want any of this burial crap. Burn me, I'll probably be going to Hell anyway."

"You're nuts." Lorne laughed.

"I know. I'm pushing the boat out to ensure you don't get bored."

"No fear of that happening."

Lorne inserted the postcode of the pharmacy into the satnav, and Sally set off.

"How are you going to approach him?" Lorne asked halfway through their journey.

"Haven't really considered it. I've been too busy going over the details that Claire gave us."

Sally's mobile rang. She nodded for Lorne to accept the call and put it on speaker. "DI Sally Parker."

"Boss, it's Joanna. I found out some very interesting information that I wanted to share with you as soon as possible, hopefully before you arrive to interview Scott Davis."

"I'm intrigued. What have you found out, Joanna?"

"He has a record for stalking a woman down in Bristol. Correction, not exactly a record. There's a blot against his name. The woman later dropped the charges. I rang the officer who dealt with the case, and he said it all happened quickly and out of the blue."

"What did? The woman dropping the charges against Davis?"

"Yes. Sergeant Finch felt that Davis got to her, threatened her in some way, but he could never prove it. Soon after, Davis left the area."

"Hmm... he must have come back here. Okay, thanks for the info, Joanna. See you later."

Lorne ended the call and dropped the phone in her lap. "Sounds like things are stacking up against him before we've even laid eyes on him."

"I'm inclined to agree with you," Sally admitted. "Do me a favour, get my spray out of the glove box, just in case we need it."

"I'm armed as well. He'd be foolish to take on both of us."

They both chuckled. Sally joined the main road, and the pharmacy was situated on the next corner.

"There's a car park on the right." Lorne pointed ahead of them.

"Got it. Okay, deep breaths. Let's see if he's on duty today."

Sally parked the car, and then they waited for the lights to change at the pelican crossing.

She opened the door to the pharmacy. There was a small queue at the counter. A petite blonde with a broad smile was dealing with the customers. Behind her, there were three steps; Sally assumed they led up to the dispensary. She could make out two people up there, a man and a woman. The other woman came down the stairs and handed a packet of medication to an old man at the front of the queue.

"We'll pretend we're browsing, give this lot a chance to clear."

They wandered down the hair colour section, and Lorne shot her a look. "Why this section? What are you trying to tell me?"

Sally grimaced. "It was a pure coincidence, I swear."

"I believe you," Lorne said unconvincingly.

They mooched up and down the aisles for around five more minutes until the final customer left the shop.

Sally approached the counter with her warrant card in hand. "Hi, I'm DI Sally Parker, and this is my partner, DS Lorne Warner. We'd like to speak to Scott Davis if he's available."

"Oh, I see. I'll ask if he has time to see you. It's always very busy around this time of day."

"Thanks."

The assistant went up the steps and had a quiet word with the man Sally had spotted up there. He glanced down at them and nodded at the assistant. She came back down the steps and with a wary smile said, "He said he can spare you a few minutes, but that's all. Come this way, I'll show you out the back to the rest room."

Sally and Lorne followed the woman through the

confined space and into a large room at the rear of the property which had a window looking out onto a bird muck-stained brick wall.

"Take a seat, Mr Davis will be with you shortly."

Lorne and Sally decided to pace the area until the door opened again and the man entered. He smiled, first at Lorne and then Sally.

"You requested to see me?"

"That's right. Thanks for agreeing to this meeting. I'm DI Sally Parker, I'm in charge of the local cold case team with the Norfolk Constabulary."

"Cold case? Should that mean something to me?"

"Shall we take a seat?" Sally asked. She gestured to the chairs running along the length of the wall.

Lorne grabbed one and positioned it next to Sally's while Davis left his where it was.

Sally shifted hers a little so she was opposite him, so she could look him in the eye during the interview. "It's to do with the Dana Caldwell case."

"I repeat, should that mean anything to me? Dana went missing years ago. I presumed her case had been closed. Don't tell me she's shown up after all these years."

"In a manner of speaking, yes, that's true."

His brow furrowed. "You've lost me. Either she's shown up or she hasn't, which is it?"

"Her remains have come to light this week, so, as far as we're concerned, her case has been reopened."

His Adam's apple bobbed and he ran a hand around his face. "What the...? Her remains? We always presumed that she had taken off, or I had. She was a law unto herself, that one. People around here thought they knew her, they didn't."

"And you did? Is that what you're telling us?"

"Yes, we shared some very intimate secrets once upon a time."

"Back when you were teenagers, is that correct?"

"That's right. I don't understand, why have you come here today?"

"To find out what you know, if anything, about her disappearance."

"Nothing. I wasn't even around here at the time she went missing. And if anyone tells you otherwise, they're leading your investigation up the garden path."

"Can you corroborate that for us?"

"Yes, of course. Want me to bring up my CV for you? Can you remind me what date she went missing?"

"Twentieth of June, twenty sixteen."

He scrolled through a file on his phone and stopped, then he angled it at Sally for her to read. "I went back to college around that time and started at the pharmacy down in Bristol on a day release."

"Was this before or after you were brought into the station for questioning regarding a stalking charge?"

He shook his head and sighed. "How did I know you were about to bring that little misdemeanour up? It was after that time. I was still relatively young when the charge was brought against me. The girl in question had initially done all the chasing in our relationship. We started going out, I told her my deepest darkest secrets, and not long after that she broke up with me and used that information against me."

"How did she do that?"

"By making up a similar situation. It was all a lie. If anything, she stalked me. I started seeing another girl after we split up, and she couldn't handle it. Her jealous streak turned nasty. She attacked my girlfriend at the swimming pool, almost drowned her, but my girlfriend refused to fight back or report her to the police. Instead, she decided to cut all ties with me, fearing for her own safety."

"And what happened with Dana? At school when you attacked her?"

"She pushed me too hard. She was nothing but a prick tease. Sorry if that's not the impression you have of her, but her friends and family have told you a pack of lies if they've omitted to tell you that she had a reputation with the boys."

Sally raised an eyebrow. "Funny how we've spoken to all her friends, and not one of them has mentioned anything of the sort."

"Because they're deluded, most of them were, from what I can recall. They're hardly going to speak ill of the dead, are they? And for the record, my heart goes out to her family. When I heard on the news that she had gone missing, I genuinely thought she had packed a bag and run off with a fella. I guess I was wrong. I'm telling you, you need to really start digging into her background to find the truth. I bet my name is mud amongst her family and friends, isn't it?"

"Actually, your name only cropped up this morning. How long have you been back in the area?"

"Only two years. Can I ask how she was killed?"

"You can, but I won't be able to tell you until the post-mortem has been conducted by the pathologist." Sally was gearing up to ask another question when her phone rang. "Sorry, I need to get this."

He shrugged. "Don't mind me, I've got nothing better to do."

She gave him a taut smile and left the room. "DI Sally Parker."

"It's Joanna. Sorry to disturb you, boss. I thought you should be aware of the news straight away."

Sally's stomach twisted into a large knot. "What news?"

"We've just heard of an assault. The victim is Michael Taylor, Dana's brother."

"Shit! How bad is he?"

"I'm not sure. He's on his way to the hospital now with stab wounds."

"Has the perpetrator been caught?"

"They tried to capture him, but he got away."

"Okay, I was about to wrap things up here, we'll get on the road. The hospital in Norwich, I take it?"

"That's it, boss."

"Thanks, Joanna. We'll shoot over there and we might as well pop in to see how Jack is at the same time, while we're there. Shit, I've just remembered, we've got Maria Adams coming in to see us at around two. Can you guys take care of that for me?"

"Of course we can. Anything specific you want us to ask?"

"No, just find out about the assault, take down her statement and let her go. It shouldn't take too long. Thanks, Jo."

"You're welcome. We're a team!"

"I'll see you later." Sally paused to reflect on what needed to be done and decided getting to the hospital instead of questioning a man who hadn't been in the area at the time of Dana's disappearance was the way forward. She reentered the room and announced, "Thanks for speaking with us. I'm afraid we're going to have to leave now. I think we've covered everything here today, but if anything else crops up, I'll be in touch with you again."

He rose from his chair, as did Lorne. She returned the chairs to the positions she'd found them in and joined Sally at the door.

"I hope nothing else crops up," Mr Davis said. "I have nothing to hide, Inspector. It's the family you should be investigating, not me."

"I can assure you, our investigation will be a thorough one. That means all parties will be interviewed fully."

"Glad to hear it. Yes, I have a misdemeanour in my past, but that was cleared up, I need you to remember that and scrub me off your suspect list, if you have one. I've turned my life around in recent years. I'm now what you would class as a respected member of the community, doing some good for the people around me. People change, I need you to bear that in mind."

"Sorry to have disturbed you today, but it was an essential part of our investigation."

"I appreciate that. I've said enough where that family is concerned. All I'm asking is that you keep an open mind."

"I will. We need to go now."

He led the way back into the pharmacy and muttered a farewell, obviously embarrassed by the intrusion in front of the rest of the staff.

Once they were outside and heading back to the car, Lorne asked, "What's going on?"

"Jo rang. She informed me that Michael Taylor has been rushed to Norwich hospital with a knife wound."

"Fuck. Is it serious?"

"She wasn't sure. I said we'd see for ourselves. We can kill two birds with one stone and check in on Jack while we're there."

"Good idea. One problem. What about Maria Adams?"

"Jo and the boys will interview her."

Lorne smiled. "I knew you'd have it covered."

CHAPTER 9

Michael Taylor had been admitted and coincidently was on the same ward as Jack. Lorne took notes while Sally asked her probing questions. Michael appeared to be a different person to the angry individual they had encountered earlier at his parents' house.

"Hello, Michael. How are you?"

"I've been stabbed, Inspector, how am I supposed to feel right now…? I'm sorry, that was uncalled for. I can't believe this has happened, I'm gutted. I pride myself on usually having my wits about me. The truth is, I thought I was safe in the bloody shower. I was wrong."

"What? Someone stabbed you while you were taking a shower?"

"That's what I just said." He stared across the ward at the two men opposite him. One had his right arm in plaster, elevated to chest height. The other man's head was bandaged, and he appeared to be unconscious.

"Where did this take place?"

"I was at the gym. I always work out during the day on a

Thursday. Someone must have known my routine and took the opportunity to pounce on me."

"Or it could have been a one-off assault. How often do you attend the gym?"

"Several times a week. I've never had any type of problem there in the past."

"Did you see the attacker?" Sally asked.

"I did, but only fleetingly. The coward wore a mask. He was quite small, he stabbed me a couple of times in the side and ran off. I shouted out for assistance but I was the only one taking a shower at the time."

"Have you fallen out with anyone at the gym lately?"

"No, never. We get a great crowd down there. I'm baffled by who would want to do this to me."

"What about away from the gym? Anyone coming to mind there?"

"No, I've been lying here trying to think, knowing that you would likely ask me that very question. I'm sorry, nothing is coming to mind at all. I had a feeling it was a dumb idea going to the gym in my free period today. I should have stayed at the school and done my workout there instead. I just needed a change of scenery, thought I would get rid of some pent-up feelings working out on the weights. We only have basic equipment at school, no weights as such. Why did I do it?"

"You mustn't blame yourself. Is there anything else you can tell us about the attacker? Did they speak?"

He stared hard at Sally and nodded.

Sally cocked an eyebrow and leaned in, waiting for his response.

"They whispered 'it was for Dana.'"

Sally and Lorne glanced at each other, both of them seemingly flummoxed by his response.

Sally's gaze shot back to Michael. "Can you think of any

reason why this person should say that?" She thought back to what Davis had told her, about not trusting the family. What was going on here? Had the family killed Dana? Did they have something to do with her disappearance?

"No, I've been lying here, it's all I've thought about since I was admitted. None of it makes any sense to me, you have to believe me."

"I do. But this attack obviously has something to do with us discovering Dana's body at the beginning of the week."

"The only thing I can think of is it's the killer covering their tracks."

Sally nodded. "Possibly. I'm going to need you to contact every member of your family, make them aware of the situation and tell them to be vigilant until we have caught this person. Do you know if the gym has any CCTV?"

"Yes, I'm sure they do. I never thought to ask. I was more concerned about my injuries."

"Understandable. Leave that to us. You just get better soon."

"Am I safe here? What if the bastard comes back to finish me off, what then? Who will protect me?"

"Don't worry. I'm sure that's not likely to happen, however, I will get onto the station and request an officer be on duty outside the ward at all times, if only to put your mind at ease."

"Thank you. I... I'm sorry for the way I spoke to you when we met the other day."

Sally smiled. "Apology accepted, and it's forgotten about. You just concentrate on your recovery and leave the rest for us to sort out."

"Thanks. God, I've yet to tell Mum, she's going to go mental. She's got enough on her plate to deal with, what with caring for Dad."

"Maybe you can count on Emma for support in the meantime."

"Yes, I'll give her a ring now. Thank you, Inspector."

"Don't worry, we'll catch the person responsible. Do you need me to call the school, let them know what's happened?"

"No, I rang the headmaster as soon as they had finished treating me and I had something concrete to tell him. He was shocked, he's not the only one, but understanding nevertheless."

"Sorry, I should have asked. What injuries did you sustain, and what's the prognosis?"

"A couple of stab wounds. I had an x-ray done, and there's a nick in one of my ribs where the blade struck. Saved by my bones, something to be proud of."

"Did you happen to see the knife? If so, can you describe it?"

"I didn't. I was too busy panicking and gasping for breath underneath the water. As you can imagine, the attacker caught me totally unaware."

"Don't worry. If there's nothing else you can tell us, we'll take a trip to the gym, see what we can find there. Feel better soon."

"I'm sure I'll be up and around again shortly. It's just the shock that I'm having trouble dealing with."

"I'm sure. It'll take time."

"I'll get there."

They said farewell and then walked the length of the ward to check on how Jack was getting on. Donna was both surprised and delighted to see them.

"I wasn't expecting to see you back so soon."

Sally pecked her on the cheek, and Lorne hugged her.

"It wasn't intentional. We had to pay a visit to someone and thought we might as well pop our heads in, see if there's any change. Have you managed to get some rest, Donna?" Sally asked.

"No rest, apart from sitting here, staring at him." She sighed heavily. "There's been no change either. Not sure what to make of that. I suppose it's too soon for there to be any improvement." She stroked the back of his hand. "I keep talking to him, hoping that my words will get through and help wake him up. But nothing!"

"It's far too early, Donna. We're going to need to be patient. His body has been through enough…" Sally abruptly stopped because the monitor went off.

She called for the nurse, but two of them were already tearing down the ward towards them.

"Leave us to it, all of you out, now."

Sally tugged on Donna's arm, and Lorne helped to guide Donna off the ward and into the corridor. Sally feared for her partner, and the feeling of uselessness and dread overwhelmed her.

Donna was in pieces. Sally insisted Donna sit down and sat in the chair next to her. She flung an arm around her shoulders and kissed the top of her head as Donna sobbed.

"I don't want him to die. Don't let them allow him to die, Sally. Get in there, order them to take care of him. He can't leave us. If he dies, I'll die with him."

"Hush, now. We don't know what's happened in there, let's not blow things out of all proportion just yet. The monitor might have malfunctioned for all we know." Sally shot Lorne a glance and shrugged. She was running out of things to say.

"Yes, that's right," Lorne chipped in, taking the hint. "There's no point getting ourselves worked up when we clearly don't know the workings of the machinery they use. There might be a sensitive alarm on it."

Just then, a doctor appeared in the hallway. He was joined

by a couple of nurses, and they all tore onto the ward. Sally's mouth dried up, the fear for her partner's life mounting by the second.

Lorne winked at her and whispered, "Stay calm. She needs us."

Sally nodded. "How are you, Donna? Looks like the reinforcements have arrived now."

"Which means it's serious, doesn't it?"

"Not necessarily. Maybe it's protocol, they all show up in force, once an alarm goes off."

"Yes, that's the likely scenario," Lorne agreed.

They sat in silence for the next few minutes until the ward door burst open and the group who had swiftly attended the scene accompanied Jack, still lying prostrate in bed, elsewhere.

Donna glanced up and stared at them. "My God, where are they taking him?"

"Don't worry, he's in safe hands. I'll see what I can find out."

Sally left her seat, and Lorne slipped into it to comfort Donna in her absence. Sally's legs wobbled as they carried her onto the ward again. One of the nurses approached her.

"Please, can you tell me what's happened to Jack? We're going frantic, not knowing."

"I'm sorry, I was about to come and break the news to you. He's suffered a cardiac arrest and has been taken up to ICU."

"What? Is he going to be okay?"

The nurse swallowed and shook her head. "I can't tell you that, it would be wrong for me to say he will be, considering his condition. I'm sure the doctor will bring you up to date at the earliest possibility."

"Oh God. How am I going to tell Donna?"

"My advice would be not to say anything at this stage."

"I can't, I won't keep her in the dark, I refuse to."

"That's up to you. His condition at present is borderline. Maybe it would be better to prepare her for the worst, just in case."

Sally's mouth hung open for a second or two until she recovered enough to turn and leave the ward again. *I feel guilty for not allowing Jack to come with us to the pub. He wouldn't be in this state if he had.*

Donna saw her coming and jumped out of her chair. "Well? Did you find out what's going on?"

"Partially. They've transferred him to ICU. They're going to work on him there, Donna. We need to remain strong. He wouldn't want to see us all hanging around here in tears, now would he?"

"It's hard. You saw the state he was in. I can't see him coming out of this, I just can't."

"Let's not go down that route, not yet. They responded quickly to the equipment once the alarm went off, that's got to be a positive that we need to cling to, Donna. Why don't I get us all a drink?" Sally had spotted a vending machine at the end of the corridor.

Lorne inclined her head. "Want me to get them?"

Sally closed her eyes, forcing back the tears, and when she opened them again, her vision was cloudy. "No, I'll get them. Coffees all round, is it?"

"I think I'll have a tea, nice and sweet for the shock, Sally, if you don't mind?" Donna asked.

"Sure. I'll be right back." Sally wandered over to the machine. She tried so hard to prevent her mind playing havoc, thinking all sorts, but failed. By the time she reached the machine, her hands were shaking uncontrollably and she was a complete mess. She gave herself a stern talking-to and inserted the first coin into the slot. She selected a white coffee but forgot to add the sugar.

Damn, get a grip, woman. Donna needs me to remain calm and positive, and I'm crumbling fast.

She dropped another coin into the machine and selected the coffee option for Lorne. This time she remembered to hit the sugar button. Then she dropped her final fifty pence into the slot and ordered Donna's tea with two sugars. Satisfied she had managed to complete her challenging task, given her current state of mind, she carried the hot cups back to her two friends.

She sipped her sugarless coffee and was almost sick. She placed it on the floor beside her. Donna stared at the wall ahead of them, sipping at her drink now and again in stunned silence.

"What if I lose him, how will I cope?" she whispered after a while.

"You can't think like that, love. Keep positive, we have to. Otherwise, it's going to drive us nuts being here. The waiting will kill us."

"I'd rather be dead if he dies. I'll never be able to raise the girls alone. I need him. *We* need him."

Sally reached for her hand and held it tightly. "Come on, don't do this to yourself, love. He's going to pull through this. We have to believe in him. He's never let us down in the past, has he?"

"No. Why do I feel so inadequate? I want to help him, but it's beyond me. Now they've whisked him away, for what? When will they tell us what's going on?"

"These things take time, you know that as well as I do, Donna. Please, bear with them, they'll give us an update as to what's going on when they can. Their priority remains with Jack, we're the least of their concerns."

Donna nodded and accepted Sally's explanation.

They sat there for the next hour or so until finally, the

doctor came to fill them in. He took them into a nearby room to share the news they'd all been dreading to hear.

"I'm sorry to have to inform you…"

Donna sobbed. Sally and Lorne stared at each other, tears filling their eyes.

The doctor continued, "Please, let me finish. Jack has suffered a heart attack. It was to be expected, given the stress his body is under at present. But we've managed to stabilise him. I refused to leave him until his body had settled down."

"What does this mean, Doctor?" Sally was the first to ask.

"It means that we're going to have to keep a close eye on him, keep him under constant observation for the next twenty-four hours. That's why we have transferred him to ICU. He'll be monitored hourly, and I'll drop in when I can."

"Will we be able to see him?" Donna said between sobs.

"You'll be able to wait outside. Or, and I think this would be for the best, you can go home and leave him to us. You need your rest as well, Mrs Blackman."

She shook her head. "I couldn't possibly leave him. If he wakes up and I'm not here, he'll think I've deserted him."

"He's not going to wake up. We've decided to keep him in a coma for the next forty-eight hours at least. We'll reassess the situation, keep a constant eye on him. You need to trust us."

"It's for the best, Donna. We can give you a lift home. You can see to the girls. They must be going out of their minds with worry, and more importantly, you can get the rest you need to battle on," Sally stated.

Donna stared at her, obviously unsure if she was talking sense or not. "Okay, I'll do it. On one proviso."

"What's that?" the doctor and Sally said in unison.

"That you call me immediately if there is any change in his condition, no matter how large or small. I need to be kept abreast of what is going on with my soulmate!"

"Of course. That goes without saying," the doctor agreed. "I'll make sure the team in ICU have your contact number. You're doing the right thing, I promise. I must get on."

"Thank you, Doctor, for everything you and the rest of the staff are doing for Jack," Sally said. She shook his hand.

He left the room, and Donna collapsed in a heap on the floor.

Sally sat beside her, hugged her and rocked her back and forth. "He's going to be all right. We have to have faith in them, Donna. We have to."

"Sally's right, Donna. We all know how determined or stubborn Jack can be. He'll be in there now, fighting to stay with us. He has everything to live for, you, the girls, his adorable granddaughter," said Lorne.

Donna sniffled and wiped her nose on a tissue. "Whom he's constantly complaining about."

"Not to me," Sally assured her. "He's besotted with the little one. Come on, my bum is numb sitting down here." She got to her feet and held out a hand to help Donna up.

"You've been amazing, both of you. I don't know what I would have done if you hadn't been here. A heart attack, at his age. If he pulls through, what will that mean for him and his career?"

"We'll consider that in the future. Let's not get bogged down with minor details such as that." Sally hooked her arm through Donna's and led her out of the room.

Lorne closed the door behind her. Sally glanced back at her and grimaced.

Lorne smiled, but it failed to reach her eyes.

CHAPTER 10

The team had done exceptionally well in their absence. Sally was in her office, casting an eye over the statement Maria Adams had given Stuart and Jordan with interest.

She joined the rest of the team in the outer office and brought the whiteboard up to date with the latest news they had gathered. "So, what have we got so far regarding the case? Two people we have already interviewed have since been attacked, Maria and Michael. In each of the attacks, the culprit mentioned Dana. What does that tell us?"

"That Dana's killer is still hanging around and is trying to intimidate the witnesses into keeping quiet?" Stuart suggested after an uncomfortable interlude.

Sally contemplated his proposal, and the more she thought about it, the more she was inclined to agree with him. "I think you're right. How do we tackle it? We can't protect all of them."

"No, but we can warn them," Lorne said. "Not flat out tell them they're at risk, but we can suggest they remain vigilant."

Sally paced the room, back and forth in front of the

whiteboard. "And what if they've heard about the two attacks that have already taken place and our call spooks them?"

Lorne tutted and hitched up a shoulder. "I haven't thought that far. It's a tough one."

"You're not wrong."

The phone on Joanna's desk rang, and she answered it.

Sally's gaze drifted in her direction when she heard the words, "When did this happen?" She marched over to Joanna's desk. She craned her neck to see what Joanna was jotting down and then tipped her head back, spun around and looked at the others.

"Emma's mother has been in an accident. This has gone too far. Make a list, split the names up and contact the rest of the people we have interviewed over the last few days. Now."

The team got to work. Lorne organised the list, and they all got on the phone.

Joanna ended the call and gave Sally the details of what had happened. "She was pulling out of her workplace, and a car rammed into the driver's door. She's okay, very shaken up. That was Emma. Maybe I should have passed the phone over to you. The trouble is, she didn't really let me get a word in."

Sally frowned. "What did she say? Was she offensive?"

"Sort of. She ranted at me, told me that the attacks on her brother and mother were down to us."

"What? How the hell does she make that one out?"

"She said that if we hadn't reopened the case into her sister's death then their lives wouldn't have been turned upside down and inside out, and the killer wouldn't have emerged again."

"What a dumb attitude to have. Get her on the phone, I'll have great pleasure in putting that woman right before the end of our shift this evening." Sally felt a hand on her arm and turned to see Lorne standing there.

"I wouldn't, not just yet. Why don't you let the dust settle overnight and get in touch with her in the morning if you still feel angry about it?"

"You think my mind will suddenly change during the evening? It ain't going to happen, Lorne. She's bang out of order, blaming us. It's as though she believes these attacks are being carried out by one of us. Nothing could be further from the truth. Bloody hell. What the fuck is going on with this investigation?"

Lorne shrugged and muttered, "Getting het up about it isn't going to help."

"It's going to make me feel a whole lot better, I can assure you."

Lorne walked back to her seat, her shoulders slumped in resignation.

Sally sighed. "I'm sorry, Lorne, you're right, of course you are, when aren't you? I'm angry that she should believe that all of this is our fault, that's all."

"I understand, but you still need to keep calm and not bite back at her. Her emotions will be upside down, it's only natural in the circumstances."

Sally's mind filled with dozens of questions, all of which concerned Emma Taylor, the main one being, "What if she's the killer?"

"Are you serious?" Lorne replied. "What proof do you have it's her?"

"No actual evidence. I'm standing here trying to understand why she had the need to attack us, that's all."

"All right, what would her motive be?" Lorne asked. "I mean, we're talking about killing her own sister here."

Sally raised a finger and wagged it from side to side. "Don't act as though I'm saying something way off the mark. We come across all sorts in the line of duty. I'm sure you've worked on cases before where sibling rivalry has been the blatant motive to the crimes committed."

Running a hand around her face, Lorne nodded. "As it happens, I have. However, it's not something that I'm willing to consider, not this time."

"May I ask why?"

Sighing, Lorne said, "I can't tell you why, except, wouldn't her brother have recognised her, while he was being stabbed in the shower?"

"And what if he had his back to the killer and just saw them fleetingly as they made their escape? He didn't tell us he saw the person, couldn't give us a description, could he? What he did tell us was that the attacker had a slight build. That could mean we're searching for a woman, couldn't it?"

"Granted. Umm… we still need to check out the CCTV footage, if there is any at the gym. We neglected to stop off there on our way back to the station."

Sally thumped her clenched fist against her thigh. "You're right. Get your stuff together, we'll drop over there now."

Lorne's gaze automatically lifted to the clock on the wall. It was already four forty-five.

"I know it's late but I wouldn't feel right leaving it until tomorrow. Don't worry, I'll go alone, I wouldn't want to put you out."

"I'm sorry, I wasn't saying that. Of course I'll come with you. What about the list? Should we still contact the other witnesses?"

"Yes, but cautiously. We'll leave the others to do it. You won't let me down, guys, will you?"

The rest of the team gave her a thumbs-up and hit the phones. Sally and Lorne gathered their jackets and handbags and bid the others goodnight, then left the room.

"I'm sorry," Lorne muttered as soon as they were out of earshot.

"For what? Challenging me?"

"Yes, I shouldn't have done that."

"Nonsense. What makes you say that? Actually, I don't want to hear it. You should know me well enough that I always appreciate a colleague's point of view, on every issue, major or minor. I refuse to go down the route of perceiving everything I think and say about a case as correct. I'm far from being a perfectionist. In fact, I've yet to meet one. Even you had your off days when you were in your prime. I'm sure you'll be the first to admit that, right?"

They reached the bottom of the stairs, and Lorne laughed.

"Admittedly, even I had my moments, and you're right, I've never considered myself a perfectionist. Pete would have backed me up on that, too. God rest his soul."

Sally pushed through the main entrance. They were a few feet from the car when she said, "You still miss him, don't you?"

She noticed the tears welling up in Lorne's eyes.

"There's never a day goes by when I don't think of him. He was a huge part of my life. All right, a pain in the rear at times, but still, they broke the mould when he was born."

Sally squeezed Lorne's arm and unlocked the car. Inside, she swallowed down the lump that had formed in her throat. "It's funny what impact certain people have on our lives without us even realising it."

"I agree. It only becomes noticeable when they're no longer with us."

"I didn't mean to upset you by bringing his name up."

"You haven't. You know, sometimes it's good to reflect on those we've lost, it makes us appreciate those around us so much more." Lorne placed her hand over Sally's and clasped it affectionately. "I know why you brought Pete's name up. You can't pull the wool over my eyes, lady. You're thinking

Jack is going to go the same way. He's not. Well, by that I mean, not now. Eventually he will, we all will… God, I know I should shut up speaking before I say something really stupid."

Sally smiled through her tears. "See, you know me better than you think you do. It suddenly hit me back there, that I could really lose him. I'm not ready to do that just yet. I'm about the same age now as you were when you lost your partner."

"Don't think about it, that's a silly comparison to make. Listen to the advice you dished out to Donna at the hospital and again when we dropped her off at home. We all need to remain positive. Considering the unthinkable should never be an alternative. He's hanging in there. When Pete left me, he didn't have a chance. He was killed outright. Jack's a fighter, and we'll all rally around to help his recovery, you'll see."

"Thanks, Lorne. You have a knack of always saying the right thing when it's needed."

"I beg to differ, but let's not analyse that one too much."

They both laughed, and Sally started the car.

WHEN THEY ARRIVED, the gym car park was heaving.

"Crap, I think we've made the wrong call, coming here at this time of night," Sally said.

"Maybe some of the locals use this place to park their cars overnight. We might as well check it out and see, now that we're here."

Reluctantly, Sally agreed, and they entered the gym. It was ultra-modern inside, lots of glass and chrome on all the fittings and fixtures.

There was a pretty brunette on duty behind the reception desk. "Hi, can I help you?"

Sally returned her smile and produced her ID. "DI Sally Parker, is the manager around?"

"Ah, yes, we've been expecting someone to drop by. I'll just let Mr Gordon know that you've finally arrived." Her hair, tied up in a ponytail, swayed like a pendulum as she walked off.

"Did I detect a snippet of sarcasm in her tone, or was that my imagination?" Sally whispered.

"You're right. Snotty cow. She probably thinks we're stuck behind a desk all day shuffling paperwork."

Sally chuckled. "We won't let her in on the secret, that most of the time we are."

The receptionist returned with a man wearing a T-shirt, exposing large biceps and tracksuit bottoms that covered what appeared to be bulging thighs. He held out a hand for Sally to shake.

"I'm Chris Gordon, I run this place. Do you want to come to my office to discuss this matter?"

"Might be a good idea, seeing how busy the gym is."

"Yes, you couldn't have shown up at a worse time."

"Sorry, it wasn't our intention to come this late. It's been an eventful day, shall we say?"

"I'm sure. We all have them. Come with me."

They followed him into his office that had a glass wall behind his desk which overlooked the vast gym. He caught Sally's mouth drop open.

"Impressive, isn't it? I designed this place myself. I can see every nook and cranny. That way I can keep an eye on the punters, ensure they're using the equipment properly and act accordingly. You know, get a member of staff to assist, if it's needed."

"Very impressive indeed. Has this place been open long?"

"Nearly five years, and I'm still paying off the loan I took out to create it." He laughed and invited them to take a seat.

"So, am I to understand that you have state-of-the-art security cameras in place?" Sally peered over his shoulder at the ceiling of the gym.

"Oh yes. Everything is top notch around here. I don't believe in doing half a job, it's all or nothing with me, always has been."

"Do you have cameras in or near the showers?"

"Not in the showers, that would be kind of indecent, wouldn't it?"

"It would. Outside then?"

"Yes, several. I've checked the footage. I'll get it up on the computer for you." He opened the drawer on his left and withdrew a laptop which he flipped open. After tapping a few keys, he swivelled it to face Sally and Lorne. "Here's Mike going into the shower. I continued to play the footage and found this person going in there after him four minutes later." He paused the footage.

Sally leant forward to get a closer look. "I can't make the person out."

The image was of an individual dressed in a dark jogging suit, the hood of which successfully shielding their features from the cameras.

"Yeah, I agree, I struggled with it, too. I checked the other cameras, and sorry to have to tell you, this is the clearest image on all of them."

"Christ, really? Not sure how that's going to help us track down the suspect. What about when they entered the gym? Any luck there?"

"Nothing. I went back an hour or so. I couldn't find anyone entering the building wearing that getup. Therefore, I reckon they must have got changed somewhere on the property, and no, it wasn't in the changing room because I've checked the footage from there already. It's a bloody mystery."

Sally raised her hands. "I hate to say this, bear with me, but could the attacker be a member of staff? I take it they probably have their own changing facilities."

"They do, and no. I'm not even going to entertain that idea. I trust my staff implicitly."

"It was just a thought, especially if the alternatives are limited."

"Whilst I agree with you to a degree, I'm also willing to put my neck on the line and vouch for every member of staff I have on my books."

"Can we get a copy of all the footage from the day? We'll take it to the lab and get them to analyse it. Maybe you missed something while you were skipping through it."

He raised an eyebrow. "Nice when a copper trusts you."

"I'm sorry if it came across that way, Mr Gordon, it wasn't my intention."

"I'm teasing you. I went ahead and made a copy, thought you might ask for one. Sorry I couldn't be more help. Will there be anything else?"

"I was hoping we could have a word with the staff, see if they heard or saw anything before the attack took place."

"I've saved you the bother. I've already asked them, and the answer was a categorical no."

"Worth a try. Okay, thanks for all your help." There was something about his cocksure attitude that wound Sally up the wrong way. "My suggestion would be to perhaps up your security around here. If word got out that someone was stabbed on your premises, you might struggle to keep hold of your clientele."

His face darkened. "Shit, I never even thought about it. You're right. What a fucking mess. Are we done here?"

"I think so. Thanks for sparing the time to see us."

He shoved the disc he'd prepared for them towards Sally, grabbed the phone on his desk and waved his hand. "You can show yourselves out, can't you? Hey, Frank, I need a word, pronto. Yes, in my office."

Sally and Lorne left the room and hung around in the reception area for the next few minutes. A man in his thirties, with a bald head and heavily sculpted muscles, knocked on Gordon's door and entered the room.

"Looks like Frank has arrived," Sally mumbled.

She stifled a grin, so did Lorne, and they left the gym.

"Can't stand having a conversation with people who have an answer for everything," Sally said.

"I totally agree. He was all calm and collected, being a smarmy shit. That soon changed once you pointed out his failure to consider the consequences. Well done, you. Ouch, I didn't mean to sound condescending."

"You didn't. Come on, let's go home."

SALLY DROPPED Lorne off and then drove the rest of the way home, her mind actively going over the events of the day. She pulled into the drive and placed her head on the steering wheel. Simon found her there half an hour later.

"What the hell? Were you asleep at the wheel? Er... you get what I mean."

Sally shook her head. "I must have dropped off." She got out of the car and stepped into the comfort of his embrace.

"My poor baby. You're exhausted. Let's get you inside."

"I'm fine. I just needed time out to take stock of what's happened today and must have fallen asleep. Enough about me, how did you get on today? Did our lot show up?"

"They did, thanks to you pushing things along for us. I questioned the neighbours to see if anyone had either seen or heard anything, and it turns out the guy next door has a camera front and back. We looked at the footage and saw two youths entering the house. Get this, he managed to supply us with a name for one of them. I've passed the details on to the uniformed officers who came out to take the statement. The guy even gave us a copy of the footage."

"That's excellent news. Maybe they're the same kids behind the other vandalism in the area as well."

"Let's hope so. I would hate to think there were more youths going around with the same intention. I have very little faith in the human race at the moment as it is."

"Yeah, you're not alone. What do you fancy for dinner?"

"I think we've both had a day from hell. Why don't I give our favourite restaurant a call and book an early table?"

"I don't think I have the energy to get all dressed up and go out. I wonder if they can supply us with a takeaway instead. I still need to take Dex for a walk yet."

"He's had a run down by the river, but I know how much you like to take him out to unwind at the end of the day. I'll give the restaurant a call, see if they can oblige. What do you fancy, if they give us the green light?"

Sally shrugged. "You choose, I'm easy... within reason. I don't fancy shellfish, though."

He pecked her on the nose. "I'll surprise you."

"And if they won't?"

"Then I'll knock up a frittata or something."

"That sounds perfect to me. Do you mind?"

"No, it's fine. Problem solved. You take Dex out and I'll crack on and prepare the veggies needed. Dare I ask how Jack is?"

"I'll give Donna a ring while I'm out with Dex and let you know when I get back."

"Sounds ominous. You'll tell me when you feel the need to confide in me."

His words stung. "I didn't mean to keep things from you. I'm sorry. Please forgive me. Jack had a heart attack when we paid him a visit this afternoon. The rest of the day has been a complete blur ever since."

He hugged her and rested his chin on top of her head. "I had no idea, how insensitive of me. Will you ever be able to forgive me?"

She pulled away from him and touched his face with her right hand. "Nothing to forgive. I was going to fill you in over dinner. I just wanted to check in with Donna first."

"You do that. Enjoy your walk with the boy. Don't be gone too long, you look dead on your feet and could do with having a few hours' rest this evening."

"I'm not about to argue with you. I'll just take him down by the river and back. It'll do us both the world of good."

She collected her furry companion, who was better now the bug he must have picked up had passed, and attached his lead. "You're still a puppy at heart, aren't you, mate?"

He gave a short sharp bark and licked her face and tugged her towards the door.

"I won't be long," she called over her shoulder before slamming the door behind her.

Once Dex relaxed on his lead, she fished her phone out of her pocket and rang Donna.

"Hello."

Sally detected Donna's exhaustion in that one word. "It's me, Sal, Donna. Just checking in to see if there's any update from the hospital."

"I rang them half an hour ago, and they told me there's no change in his condition. I'm not sure what to think about that."

"Look on the bright side, we have to. At least his condition hasn't worsened since we left the hospital."

"I suppose so."

"How are the kids holding up?"

"It's mood swing central around here. I think we're all on tenterhooks and snapping at each other, I'm including myself in that as well. I feel bereft, lost without him. I glanced at the clock a little while ago and told myself he'll be walking through the door any second, wanting to know what's for dinner."

"It's hard, I know. And what is on the menu for dinner for you and the girls? You need to keep your strength up."

"Don't worry, we won't starve. I've been in the kitchen since you dropped me off. I've baked a sponge, and there's a casserole bubbling away in the oven. It helped to take my mind off what's going on back at the hospital."

"That sounds delicious."

"You're welcome to join us, I think I've made enough to feed everyone down at the station."

"Aww… the offer is appreciated, but Simon has got our dinner all in hand. I'm out walking Dex."

"You've got a good man there, Sal."

"Don't I know it? When was the last time Jack cooked you a meal?"

"I don't even have to pause to think about that because the answer is never." She laughed. "In fact, I'll go as far as to say that I don't think he even knows where the kitchen is situated in our house."

"Never. That can't be right."

"Take my word for it. It's true."

They both laughed, and Sally felt relieved to hear Donna so upbeat, given the state she'd left her in when she'd dropped her at home earlier.

"That's the spirit. Keep your chin up, love, if only for the girls. Have they asked if they can visit him?"

"Yes, it was the first thing out of their mouths. I told them they wouldn't want to see him the way he is. I'm not sure if that was the right or wrong thing to say, judging by their reaction and how they've played me up ever since. What would you do in my shoes, Sally?"

"I believe this is one of those occasions where you're going to feel damned if you do and damned if you don't. Maybe see how he is in the morning and take it from there. I can understand them wanting to see him, it's whether they can handle the truth when it hits them full in the face. Thinking back to when I was their age, my inquisitive nature got the better of me on several occasions, and I felt punished for it."

"Oh, tell me more."

"My father had a bad accident with a forklift truck on a building site once. They had to sew one of his arms back on... God, I don't think Jack even knows about this."

"Jesus, and that occurred when you were a child?"

"About sixteen. I persuaded Mum to let me visit him at the hospital, and I have to tell you, I was physically sick when I first laid eyes on him. I've kind of hated hospitals ever since."

"Oh heck. I can fully understand you feeling that way. A bad experience like that can leave an indelible mark in our minds."

"Seeing him lying unconscious in that hospital bed haunted my dreams for years. I've been expecting all those bad feelings to come surging back during my visits to see Jack, but thankfully, so far, I've managed to keep them under control."

"Maybe you've given me the answer without even realising it. I'm going to keep the girls away from the hospital, at least until he wakes up."

"It might be for the best."

"Mum, where's my school shirt?" one of the girls shouted in the background.

"I'd better go. They rarely see what's sitting on the hanger before their very eyes. I'll call you if anything changes with Jack. Thanks for ringing, Sally."

"Always here for you, don't ever forget that, Donna."

"I won't. You're a good friend."

"Sending love and hugs to all of you. Go easy on yourself."

She ended the call and patted Dex on the head. "I'm lucky to have you, boy. Shall we go home and get some dinner?"

He licked his lips, and she laughed.

"And they say animals are stupid. You're more intelligent than a lot of people I know, but I wouldn't tell anyone else that. Come on."

They turned and walked home.

Simon had the dinner ticking over nicely when they got there. By the time she had fixed Dex's dinner and put down fresh water for him, her husband had dished up and poured them both a glass of wine.

During the delicious but simple meal, she relayed what Donna had told her.

"Bugger. I have to ask why Jack wasn't in ICU in the first place."

"Funny you should say that, Lorne said the same. I don't know how these things work, how ill a person has to be to get a bed on the unit. Still, there's nothing we can do about it now. He's in the best possible place for him. I'm thinking it's a good thing he's been put in an induced coma, right?"

"Normally I would agree with you. We're going to have to see how it pans out for Jack. His body is obviously under a fair amount of stress right now, so it makes sense to me. Let's hope they're monitoring him closely and not just saying they are, because if he has another heart attack, I'm not sure his body will survive next time."

Sally dropped her knife on the table. "God, really? Why did you have to tell me that?"

"Sorry, I thought we were discussing the situation openly. Forget I said anything."

"That's going to be pretty bloody hard, Simon."

He winced, and they both finished off their glasses of wine before Sally spoke again.

"I'm exhausted. I'll do the washing up and go to bed."

"Go. I'll shove it all in the dishwasher, it can wait until tomorrow. I'll be up soon. I have a few pieces of paperwork to sort out for the insurance people before I can join you."

She left the table and kissed him. "Good luck. Thanks for dinner."

"My pleasure, as always. Sorry I opened my big mouth and put my size tens in it as far as Jack's concerned."

"You didn't. It's always best to be prepared. I was on the fence about his condition anyway. Let's hope he proves us both wrong and pulls through okay."

Dex followed her out of the kitchen and up the stairs. She had a quick shower and fell asleep as soon as she turned the light out.

CHAPTER 11

The first thing Sally did the following morning, after letting Dex in the garden, was give Donna a call. "Hi, it's me. Any news, love?"

"I rang the hospital fifteen minutes ago. They told me he'd had a comfortable night and everything was looking far more positive, although he's far from out of the woods yet."

Sally let out the breath she'd been holding in and leaned against the doorframe. "What a relief, you must be thrilled."

Donna laughed. "I wouldn't go quite that far, but yes, I'm feeling far happier than I was yesterday, that's for sure."

"Good. As I keep telling you, he's a fighter. He's got this, and so have you, Donna. I'm going to get ready for work now. Give me a shout if you need me at all."

"I will. Thanks for checking in with me, Sal. Have a good day."

"Well, that's debatable with a killer on the loose."

They both laughed, and she ended the call to find Simon had crept up behind her.

She fell into his arms. "That was Donna. He's had a good night."

"There you go. All that worrying for nothing. You were tossing and turning all night. Are you sure you're up to go to work this morning?"

"I will be if someone cooks me one of their supersized breakfasts."

He smiled and pecked her on the nose. "Say no more. I could do with one of those myself. You go and get dressed and leave the rest to me. I'll deal with Dex."

She didn't need telling twice.

HALF AN HOUR LATER, feeling replete and ready for what the day had to throw at her, workwise, Sally drove into work. She flashed her lights at the car in front of her as she joined the main road. Lorne raised a hand and stuck her thumb up.

Sally did the same. A few minutes later, they arrived at the station.

"Have you heard how Jack is?" Lorne said.

"He's had a comfortable night, and Donna was feeling far more positive when I spoke to her earlier."

"That's great news. He'll be back, being grouchy around here in no time at all."

"Let's hope so. Right, I need to give that Emma Taylor a call first thing, and before you ask, no, I haven't calmed down overnight. I'm still incensed by her having a go at Joanna."

"All right. I've offered up my advice, it's up to you whether you act upon it or not, you're the boss."

"Don't make me out to be the bad guy in all of this."

"I'm not trying to. All I want to remind you is about the turmoil the family must be going through. Dana has been missing for six years. That would take a toll on anyone's emotions, yours and mine included, wouldn't it?"

"I guess you're right. Why are you always the smartest one on the block about this kind of thing?"

"Years of experience of dealing with a vast number of people from all walks of life, from drug dealers to vicars and anything in between."

Sally smiled. "I'm glad you're my partner on this one, Lorne, we understand each other and bounce off each other."

"Hey, Jack's not all bad. He has his good days."

"Yeah, the last one was back in twenty twenty when he bought me a bacon sandwich at a greasy spoon."

Lorne planted a friendly punch on her arm. "You're a card when you want to be. Keep that frame of mind when speaking to Emma and you'll go far."

Sally raised an eyebrow. "You reckon? We'll soon see."

They entered the station to discover they were the first to arrive. Lorne switched on the computers, and Sally stuck her head into her office. Relieved to see her desk empty, she made her way over to the drinks station to make the coffees.

"I'll need this down my neck before I tackle ringing the lady with her hand up her arse."

The rest of the team drifted in. Once everyone had made themselves a coffee, Sally asked how each of them had got on the previous evening, calling the other witnesses.

"I had an interesting conversation with your friend Liz yesterday," Joanna said. She placed her mug on the desk and searched for her notes.

"Go on. In what way?" Sally asked.

"She told me that she thought someone had been in her rear garden, but when she had a look around, she decided to put it down to her overactive imagination."

"Interesting. She could be right. Did she mention if she was back at work yet?"

"Yes, she said she started back yesterday but only managed a couple of hours. Her boss sent her home at around four."

"We'll bear that in mind. Did you tell her to get in touch if anything else happens?"

"I did."

"Okay, I've built up enough courage, I'm going to give Emma a call in my office."

"Good luck," Lorne said.

"Thanks, hopefully, I won't need it."

Sally reached her chair and was about to pick up the phone when it rang, startling her. "Hello, DI Sally Parker, how may I help?"

"Inspector, it's Rob Caldwell."

"Hello, Rob. Is everything all right?" She detected a note of anxiety in his tone.

"I... I don't know how to say this but..."

"Come right out with it, Rob. What's troubling you?" Her heart raced. *Is he about to make a confession?*

"I was on my way out this morning, Abby had already left for work, and, well, I was attacked."

"Attacked? Are you all right?"

"Yes, luckily I had my wits about me and was able to fight this person off. They dropped a weapon, and I'm not sure what to do with it."

"Weapon? What type of weapon?"

"A knife."

"Are you at home?"

"Yes. I'm too shaken up to drive."

"Don't worry. I'll be there in fifteen minutes. Don't touch the knife. We'll need it for evidence."

"I used a tissue I had in the car to bring it into the house."

"Good man. Keep the doors locked and put the kettle on. I've got a few things I need to tell you when I get there."

"Oh God, do you know who the killer is? Was the killer here today? The person who tried to kill me? Should I be worried?"

"I'll answer all your questions when I get there. Lock all the doors. Ring Abby. Ensure she remains safe without scaring her."

"Christ, how the hell am I going to do that?"

"You'll think of a way. I'll see you soon."

Sally stormed out of the room and into the outer office. "Lorne, we're off out. Rob Caldwell was attacked by someone this morning. They dropped the weapon. We're going to shoot over there and pick it up. I need the rest of you to ring everyone on the list again, barring the family. Leave them to me. We'll drop over there this morning while we're out, reiterate everyone's need to remain vigilant, without spooking them. The killer obviously has an agenda. We need to nip it in the bud before they put someone else in hospital."

Sally and Lorne tore out of the office and down the stairs, almost bumping into DCI Green in the process.

"Sorry, sir. Can't stop, it's an emergency."

"Very well, I'll expect an update ASAP upon your return, Inspector."

"You'll get one, don't worry." Sally grunted as she jumped off the bottom step. "As if I haven't got enough on my plate," she complained.

"You know what male bosses are like, they feel neglected if you don't keep them informed."

"I had noticed over the years."

SALLY COULD TELL that Rob was still badly shaken up by what he'd been subjected to that morning.

"Coffee?" he asked, the second they set foot inside the house.

"Why don't I make it while you sit down and have a chat with the inspector?" Lorne suggested.

He nodded. The three of them went through to the

kitchen. Sally and Rob sat at the table while Lorne prepared the mugs with milk and sugar and waited for the kettle to boil.

Sally sat next to Rob. "Can you tell me exactly what happened, Rob?"

"It's probably my fault. I was too busy reading a message on my damn phone from my boss to notice this person approaching me. I'd almost reached the car. This individual walked up to me, and I suddenly saw their arm jerk towards me, or jab, I suppose is the right term. My reaction was to pull my stomach in and jump back. If I hadn't, the knife would have caught me in the abdomen. I tussled with this person, managed to karate chop the knife out of their hand, and they ran off. I was in two minds whether to chase after them or not, but my legs were that wobbly, I don't think they would have carried me too far."

"Don't worry, you've got the weapon. Did you notice if they were wearing gloves or not?"

"Yes, they were. Black patent or leather ones. That's going to scupper your ability to get a print off the knife now, isn't it?"

"Don't worry. It depends if the knife has been newly bought or if the perpetrator has used it before, without wearing their gloves."

"Let's hope so."

"Did they say anything when they struck?" Sally asked.

Lorne poured the water into the mugs, stirred them and delivered the drinks to the table and sat beside Sally.

"They said, in a gruff voice, 'this was for Dana'. I think those words shook me up more than the attack did, if I'm honest with you."

"Okay, I need to bring you up to date on a few things."

"You said as much over the phone. What's been going on, Inspector? Do you know who this person is?"

"Unfortunately, we don't, not right now. I have to tell you that I'm presuming the same person has struck in the past few days."

"Struck? You mean other people have been attacked? Such as who?"

Sally reeled the attacks off one by one. "My team had the task of calling everyone on the witness list, warning them to remain vigilant."

He frowned and stared at his mug. "Why didn't someone have the decency to give me a ring at the same time? You don't still believe I had anything to do with Dana's death, do you? Because that's how it's coming across to me."

"No, nothing could be further from the truth, I promise. It was merely an oversight on our part. We concentrated on the witnesses and the family." The more Sally spoke, the more she realised that she and the team had messed up, big time. "Please accept my apologies."

"You know what I'm getting from this? That all this could have been prevented, if only you had informed me."

"You're right. If you want to issue a complaint about how you believe the investigation has been handled, I won't step in your way."

"Why would I do that? What use would it serve to piss off the leading officer working on my wife's case?"

"I won't let you down again, I swear I won't."

"I hope for your sake you don't. "Jesus. Yes, I can't believe what I'm sodding hearing, you should have informed me if Abby's life and mine were in danger."

"I know. I realise now that I probably made the wrong call, I should have contacted you myself." Sally's gaze drifted over to the worktop to the side of her. "Is that the knife?"

"Yes, I put it in a freezer bag, I hope I did the right thing?"

"You did." She stood and examined the weapon. "My

trained eye tells me that this is an ordinary kitchen knife, probably from a set."

"I thought the same. So all you have to do is knock on millions of doors to see who has a knife missing."

She returned to her seat and smiled. "If only it were that simple and we had the resources to do it."

"So what's the answer?"

"At this stage, I wish I knew. Our main priority is getting the weapon to the lab for them to carry out the necessary tests on it. If this person's prints are on the knife and they match to someone on our database, then it's job done."

"And if they don't?" Rob countered.

"We'll cross that bridge when we get to it. Our aim right now is to keep everyone safe. Has anyone been in touch with you? Either a member of Dana's family or any of her friends in the past few days?"

"No one, except Maria. Funny she didn't mention that she had been attacked."

"How did the conversation go?"

"She wanted to drop by and see Abby and me, when it was convenient. I had a lot of meetings planned for this week, change of season in the trade, so we're at our busiest at this time of the year. We agreed to leave it until the weekend. We arranged for her to come over and have a spot of lunch with us on Saturday."

"That's nice of her, to check on you both, especially as she's one of those who has been attacked."

"I thought so as well. It's more than Dana's family have done."

"Something else cropped up during our investigation that I need to run past you, Rob."

His brow wrinkled. "Go on."

"We tracked down one of Dana's ex-boyfriends. He had a lot to say about Dana, and none of it was pleasant."

"Who was it?"

"Scott Davis, do you know him?"

"That scumbag. Yes, I know of him, although I've never actually met the bastard. I knew they had a history. What did he say about Dana?"

"That she often played around, is that true?"

"No, not as far as I know. Of course, I can only speak for myself. I wasn't aware of her cheating on me, if that's what you're asking. Cheeky gobshite. He was kicked out of school for harassing her. Are you really willing to take his word as gospel?"

"It's something we can't ignore. If you believe Dana was faithful, then that's good enough for me."

Sally had put her phone on silent, and it vibrated on the table next to her. She picked it up and stared at the caller ID. It was the station, more importantly, a member of her team. She peered over her shoulder and eyed the back door. "Excuse me, I need to take this."

"Be my guest. You either take it in the lounge or go in the garden, the choice is yours."

"Had it been raining, I would have opted for the first choice, but if it means I'll get the opportunity of getting an early tan, I'll elect to go outside instead." She raced to the door and answered the call. "Joanna, what's up?"

"Sorry to disturb you, boss. Emma's been on the phone again, blasting me for not returning her call."

"Shit. Okay, we're nearly through here. Where is she, did she say?"

"At her mother's house. She's taken a few days off work to look after her parents."

"We'll be there in half an hour. Sorry you had to take the flack again, hon."

"I don't mind. I wanted you to be on your guard, that's all."

"We'll call round there and then stop off at the lab on our way back."

"Okay, boss. See you later."

Sally slotted her mobile in her pocket and joined Lorne and Rob once more in the kitchen. "Sorry about that, it couldn't have been avoided. Are we done here now?"

Rob stared at her. "I don't know, are we? Do you think the person who attacked me is likely to come back? Are you going to be offering any type of protection for either me or Abby?"

"My first thought would be that this person wouldn't dare show their face around here again. I believe they'll think that we'll put an officer on guard outside your house. Unfortunately, we don't have the resources to protect every Tom, Dick or Harry who has ever had a threat made against them. You're going to need to always remain vigilant, at least until we've caught the suspect."

He shook his head and tutted several times. "I can't believe you're allowing this lowlife to get away with this."

"I'm not. I've got no idea where you got that impression. I'm sorry you're not willing to accept things as they are, there's very little I can do to alter that. Sergeant, we need to get on the road now."

He jumped to his feet. "Where are you going?"

"To Dana's parents', to have a word with Emma."

He folded his arms and tapped his foot. "So you're giving their safety precedence over mine? Is that what this boils down to?"

"We're treating everyone the same. I'm pleading with you not to think otherwise."

Defeated, he showed them to the front door without saying another word.

Sally felt the waft of the door being slammed behind her the second she set foot outside the house.

"Jesus, not how we wanted that to end, eh?" Lorne muttered.

"I'm used to people having a go at me, even though it pisses me off when all I'm trying to do is bust a gut for these people in the first place."

"Ignore them and just keep going. This case isn't getting easier, it's getting more and more difficult to navigate with each passing day, Sal. That's down to the killer's agenda, not anything we have done, either rightly or wrongly. I need you to keep that in mind."

"Thanks, Lorne. You know how to keep me grounded. That was Joanna on the phone, informing me that Emma had called the station again, full of angst."

"God help us when we get there. She needs to calm down before she self-destructs."

"I can see it from her point of view, with both her brother and mother being involved in incidents, but she needs to let us get on with the job in hand and stop bloody badgering us every five minutes."

"Are you going to tell her about the incident with Rob?"

"I'm not sure just yet. Maybe I should. Perhaps she'll reconsider his part in her sister's murder if I do. And if I don't…"

"It's another tough one to call. I feel for you."

"What would you do in my shoes?"

They got back in the car, and Sally pulled away when a gap in the traffic became available.

"I wouldn't hold back. I'd let her know every single detail, within reason, if only to get her off my back."

"Really, you think that's likely to work?"

"Who knows when someone is that worked up about the case?"

"In her defence, I reckon she has a reason to be. Shall I give her a call, tell her we're on our way?"

"Why not, you might as well."

SALLY PARKED the car and drew in several steadying breaths before she and Lorne exited the vehicle to face the music.

Emma had been watching out for them. She opened the door and urged them to get inside and slammed the door shut behind them.

"Are you all right, Emma? Has anything else happened to your parents today?"

"No. I'm anxious. I'm determined to do everything I can to keep us all safe, but you need to lend us a hand, too. Where were you? I've been frantic, going out of my mind. I thought you were going to get back to me last night, and here we are, almost halfway through the day, and you're only just showing up at our door."

"I'm sorry you feel that way, Emma. We've been at Rob's."

"Him! Why with him and not us? Why? I demand to know!" she insisted, her tone getting angrier with every word.

"Emma, give them a chance," Jane Taylor said from the door to the lounge. "At least invite them in first before jumping all over them."

"I'm sorry. Mum's right, please forgive me. Come through to the lounge."

She led the way, and Sally and Lorne shared a concerned look. They joined Emma and her mother, who were clutching hands and sitting on the sofa.

"How are you, Jane?" Sally asked. She sat next to Lorne in one of the two armchairs opposite.

"I'm over the shock now. I wouldn't wish that on anyone, being shunted like that, when it was least expected."

"I'm sorry you had to go through that. Did you see the driver of the vehicle?"

"No. And there's no point in you asking me if I recognise the make of the car either. It all happened too quickly for me to take everything in." She held her shaking hand up. "I've never been so terrified before, ever."

"We're trying to locate footage from the cameras in the area. So far, it's proving difficult."

"Why?" Emma asked.

"Because not every shop has CCTV. They should, we believe it should be made law. Sadly, it isn't. Until we view what actually occurred, there's nothing we can really do about it. I know that's not what you want to hear right now."

"Why were you with him?" Emma demanded to know.

Sally obtained eye contact with the woman and shot from the hip. "Because he was attacked this morning."

"What?" Emma screeched while her mother gasped and slapped a hand over her mouth.

"That's right. We're not wasting time on this investigation, if that's your belief, Emma. We're dealing with different aspects of it as they arise."

"So why didn't you come and see Mum yesterday after her prang in the car? Why give him the priority over us?"

Sally took a moment's pause and admitted, "You're right, we should have come out last night. I'm not using this as an excuse, but it was an exceptionally long day, and we had to contend with bad news about a colleague."

"Like we give a shit about that," Emma snapped back.

"Emma! Shut up. Stop being so heartless. We have no reason to suspect the inspector and her team aren't doing their very best for us." Jane faced Sally and smiled. "I hope your colleague is okay?"

"His life is hanging in the balance, but we're dealing with it. Just like we're giving our all to the case. DS Warner is now my acting partner, she has over twenty-five years' service under her belt with the Met Police. We're using that to our advantage."

"If that's the case, then why haven't you caught the suspect yet? How many more frigging people is he going to be allowed to attack? How many lives will he successfully turn upside down before you pull your finger out and arrest him?" Emma demanded.

"We're doing our very best," Sally assured her.

"But are you, though?" Emma tutted. "Do you even know who the killer is yet? We've had no update on your progress so far, so forgive me for believing that you've put the investigation on the backburner. Maybe we should get someone else to run it for us, you know, if you're too distracted by what's going on with your colleague, to be bothered about the investigation."

Sally sensed Lorne was about to jump to her defence and nudged her with her knee. "Had this not been a cold case we're dealing with, you'd be within your rights to seek another team to assist you. However, I have to inform you, you're stuck with us. I'm sorry if you feel we've failed you up until now. I don't see it that way. To date, we've reinterviewed all the witnesses and dealt with a couple of incidents that we couldn't have foreseen taking place, like the attack on your brother."

"There, listen to the inspector, Emma. I believe, and so should you, that she is doing her very best for us. Let's not make her job harder than it needs to be." Jane clutched her daughter's hand and squeezed it.

"All right. I'm sorry," Emma mumbled. "Where do we go from here?"

"We keep trying to obtain proof and evidence against the perpetrator. We've already tracked down a significant person from Dana's past who we intend keeping a close eye on." Sally kicked herself for not organising surveillance on

Davis, in light of what had taken place since she had spoken to him.

Her mobile rang, disrupting the conversation. Sally removed it from her pocket, nodded at Lorne and excused herself from the room.

"Joanna, this is becoming a regular occurrence. What's up?"

"We've received a call from Liz Baddock's neighbour. She was pretty distraught, boss."

"Was she? Why?"

"She said she looked out of her window, after hearing some kind of commotion, to see Liz being bundled into a car."

"Shit! Here we go again. What type of car?"

"The neighbour got the reg number for us, and I'm not sure how to tell you this, but the car belongs to…"

"Christ, don't stop there, for fuck's sake, tell me."

"Sorry, one of the guys distracted me. Maria Adams."

"What? I wonder what's going on. Why would she bundle Liz into her car…? Unless… fuck, I'm being slow on the uptake here, aren't I? She's the killer. Fuck, fuck and triple fuck. She must be, she was the one who was with Dana the night she went missing. All right, put a frigging alert out on her car."

"Already done, boss, Jordan actioned it as I was calling you."

"Good to see you're all on the ball in my absence. Okay, we'll finish up here and get back to the station. Can you hit the phones in the meantime, Joanna? Ring all the other witnesses, those who were Maria's friends, and ask if they know of anywhere she is likely to want to go to be alone."

"I'll make sure we cover that right away, boss. Jordan is tracking the car through the ANPR now."

"Keep me abreast on that front. TTFN." Sally ended the

call and raced back into the lounge. She held up a warning finger and said, "I don't have time for any arguments, you're going to have to trust me on this one, Emma. I've had a call from my team, informing me that Liz has been abducted."

"What? How?"

Sally wagged her finger. "I don't have the time to analyse it. What I need to know is if you can think of anywhere Maria Adams goes when she needs time to herself."

"What? Why...? Shit! You're not telling me that Maria is the one who has taken Liz, are you?"

"Yes. Think, it's really important. If she's the one who killed your sister, then every second counts, and we're up against it."

Emma sobbed and covered her face with her shaking hands. "No, no, no. I can't believe this... shit, why didn't I think about that? Why?"

Sally dropped to the floor in front of Emma and tore her hands away. "What? What are you saying? Do you know where she's taken her?"

"No, I wish I did, but I've just remembered that Maria often spoke about a relative she used to visit in Feltwell."

"What the...? Jesus, and you didn't think to mention this at the start of the investigation?"

"Don't blame me," she screeched in Sally's face. "I was in shock. My sister's remains had just been found, my head was all over the fucking place, and then my brother and mother were both caught up in incidents. I haven't had time to breathe properly, let alone mull things over, searching for damn clues."

"I'm sorry. I had no right castigating you. Can you think of anywhere else she might go? We can pretty much guarantee that she won't take Liz back to her place. What about a boyfriend, has she got one even?"

"No. She dumped Patrick not long after Dana went

missing and hasn't trusted another bloke again since. She's a bit of a loner, that one. I'm sorry, we weren't what I'd call bosom buddies, ever. We tolerated each other on nights out with the others, nothing more. You need to get out there and find her. If she's already killed Dana, there's no telling what she might do to Liz. Liz isn't well, you have to help her, please!"

"Will the others know where she might take Liz?"

"I don't know. I can't speak for anyone else."

Sally hoisted herself to her feet by placing a hand on her partner's knee. "Come on, let's go. I'll be in touch soon. Keep the doors locked until you hear from me," Sally shouted then bolted out the door and up the path towards the car.

"I can't believe it," Lorne huffed out once they were in the vehicle. "She was at the damn hospital the other day, telling us that she had been attacked. What about her fingers?"

"What about them? She could have done that herself, to put us off the scent. Fucking bitch has played us from the beginning of this investigation and been laughing behind these good peoples' backs for effing years. I need to call Australia. What's the time over there?"

"Around eleven at night. Go for it, sod what time it is."

Sally looked up the number she had for Charles Langdon and rang it.

"Why don't you make the call and I'll drive?" Lorne offered.

They switched places, and Lorne got on the road, heading back to the station.

"Yes, Charles, I'm so sorry to disturb you at this time of night. This is DI Sally Parker from the UK again, we spoke the other day."

"No bother. We were having a barbie. When in Oz and all that. What's wrong?"

"I have a simple question to ask you. Do you know a Maria Adams?"

"Yes, of course I do. She's my second cousin. Why?"

"We believe she has abducted a woman with intent to harm her. We also believe that she is the person who dumped the body we found at your house the other day."

"Christ, really? Mind you, I shouldn't be surprised. She was always an odd girl growing up."

"May I ask in what way?"

"Just kind of distant, although she got on well with my gran."

"Did she have a key to the property?"

"Possibly. If she did, I wasn't aware of it. Christ, what happens now?"

"Thank you. Now we just need to find her. This might be asking a lot, but do you know any other places Maria might take the woman she has kidnapped? Obviously your place will be out of bounds at the moment. SOCO won't have finished searching for further evidence."

"Sorry, no way I'd know that type of thing."

"Don't worry. Thanks for taking my call." She hung up and rested her head back against her seat. "I hate being duped. There's nothing worse. Am I guilty of taking my eye off the ball, you know, what with Jack's predicament?"

"If you're guilty of it then so are the rest of the team. Don't feel bad, Sal. She's good at what she does, the art of deception. She's an expert at it after all these years. What a sick woman to do that to her friend and then to remain friends with the rest of them. Maybe she got off on them falling to pieces."

"More than likely. Name me a killer who isn't unhinged in some way. No, I shouldn't have said that out loud, not with Liz's life hanging in the balance, prodding at my damn conscience."

"You're nuts. There's no way we could have worked all this out before now. Maybe if we had known Maria was Langdon's relative from the outset it would have been a different story. She's canny, Sal, and as much as it grieves me to say, she's good at what she does. Let's leave it there, shall we? Up until now, she hasn't killed anyone else. We need to keep that uppermost in our minds."

"What are you saying, that she's losing her touch after all these years?"

"She's rusty, let's call it that for now. Which should give us hope that Liz will come through this."

Sally's phone rang in her lap. She answered it on the second ring. "DI Sally Parker."

"Boss, it's Jordan. I've got eyes on the vehicle."

"What? Well done, Jordan. Where are they?"

"Going south on the A11, heading towards Thetford."

Sally and Lorne quickly glanced at each other. "She's going back to the house. She's deluded if she thinks SOCO will have processed the scene yet. Alert the team at the house, also get every patrol car in the area on her tail. We'll shoot over there now. Keep me updated if anything else comes to light, Jordan. Good work, stick with it."

"Yes, boss."

Sally threw the phone back into her lap and sighed. "She's within our grasp. I hope we don't screw this up, for Liz's sake."

"PMA, Sal."

* * *

As promised, Jordan kept them informed with every move Maria made. As yet, she had escaped capture, but Sally had a positive feeling running through her. It was only a matter of time before the net closed in on Maria, and she was determined that she and Lorne would be there, front and centre, when it did.

"Don't hold back, Lorne, you have my permission to give her some welly, she can take it."

Lorne laughed. "Takes me back to the days I used to chase all the hardened criminals around London. Never dreamed I'd be doing the same up here."

"It goes with the territory, I mean, being a copper in today's society."

Sally's phone rang. She picked it up and dropped it again. "Ouch, this baby is hot today."

They both laughed.

"Answer it, you idiot," Lorne said.

"DI Sally..."

"Boss, it's Jordan. The car approached the house, and two SOCO guys tried to yank the driver's door open and tackle her, but she got the better of them and drove off."

"Fuck, she knows we're onto her now. Put your foot down, Lorne, that's an order. Jordan, get everyone on the team out on the road and keep in touch. Use your blues and twos, there's no point in any of us trying to be discreet now."

"We'll get on it, boss. Do you want Joanna to man the phones here?"

"Yes, if she's okay with that."

"She is, boss. Talk soon."

Sally ended the call and motioned for Lorne to go hell for leather. "Come on, partner, I want to be the one who nails this bitch's arse to the wall."

"That makes two of us. Hang on tight."

The adrenaline pumped the closer they got to the house. Lorne drew up. One of the SOCO guys was getting something out the back of his van.

Sally lowered the passenger window and shouted, "Which way did she go and how long?"

"Five, maybe six minutes. She went that way. We did our best but…"

"Don't worry. Thanks for at least trying."

The tyres squealed, and Sally whooped for joy at the speed they were going, disregarding any thought of crashing, not with an experienced advanced driver like Lorne behind the wheel.

The signs for Thetford Forest caught Sally's attention up ahead.

"Are you thinking what I'm thinking?" Sally asked.

"Want me to pull over, see if we can spot her car?"

"Yes, to me, it's the only option left open to us."

Lorne drove up and down the rows of cars. It was a sunny day, so there were dozens of people taking advantage of the great outdoors at their disposal.

Sally sat forward and jabbed her finger. "There, that's the car, I'm sure of it. There's an entrance into the woods off to the left. Let's set off and see what we can find."

"I'll get in touch with the others. Let them know where we are."

"I was just about to do it. I'll use the group chat on my phone."

Lorne locked the car, and they set off into the woods. Unfortunately, they were on their own after the reception dipped.

"Shit. Not what we needed at all," Sally cursed.

"It doesn't matter. I can hear them getting closer in the distance."

They upped their pace, scanning the area on either side of them as they followed the path through the dense forest. They passed several couples walking dogs.

Sally took a punt and stopped to talk to a man and woman in their fifties. "Sorry to disturb your walk." She flashed her ID. "Have you passed two females, both appearing a bit anxious perhaps?"

"Yes, they went past us just around the corner at the top there," the man said. "Is everything all right? One of the women had tears in her eyes, and the other one was holding on tightly to her arm. We thought she'd had some bad news, but now that you've raised the point about them both seeming anxious, yes, I'd have to say they definitely fit the bill."

"Thanks, that's great."

Sally and Lorne broke into a trot. Meanwhile, the sirens had died down around them. That could only mean one thing, that the troops weren't far behind them.

"Keep your eyes open, they might stray from the path if Maria's anxiety levels increase."

Lorne nodded. "Every possibility. Shit, we didn't bring a Taser with us."

"I should have asked the team to ensure they signed a couple out. It's too late now. We'll have to combat the bitch between us."

"That's doable." Lorne grinned at Sally and rubbed her hands. "Bring it fucking on!"

They pressed on, and within a few minutes they were joined by the rest of the team, and it was Jordan who spotted Liz and Maria. Sally brought the team to a halt and sent them off in different directions with strict instructions to wait for her orders before approaching either of the women.

She watched the team disperse and sucked in a steadying breath.

"You've got this, and I'm right behind you, so *we've* got this, Sal. Don't ever think otherwise."

Sally nodded and smiled at her partner. "Then what are we waiting for? Let's go bring the fucking murdering bitch down."

Lorne punched the air, and they set off through the trees, taking the same route as Maria and Liz had moments earlier. The women were out of sight by now, but it wasn't long before Lorne drew Sally's attention to a flash of colour in the distance.

"There, behind that large tree. She obviously knows we're around."

"Why don't I announce myself, keep Maria occupied, and you double round the back, jump her if the opening arises?"

"Sounds good to me. I've got my spray in my pocket and I'm not afraid to use it."

"The rest of the team are around, somewhere. They should be within spitting distance of us at all times."

"Peace of mind is a great asset. I'll go right."

"Be careful."

"Goes without saying. Ditto, matey."

Sally issued a thumbs-up, swallowed down the saliva filling her mouth and took a few steps closer to the huge oak tree. "Maria, the game is up. I can see you. Why don't you bring Liz out into the open?"

"Fuck off. You'd be wise to back off and let us get out of here."

"Why would I do that? We both know what you did all those years ago. Come out and face the consequences."

Sally's words obviously struck home, because a few seconds later, Maria stepped out from behind the tree with Liz. Sally's intestines knotted when she saw the knife Maria was holding against Liz's neck.

Sally placed her hands out in front of her. "Now there's no need for it to end this way. Why don't you let Liz go? This is between you and me, Maria. Liz is an innocent bystander in all of this."

"She deserves to die, they all do. None of you know the truth about Dana." The blade nicked Liz's throat.

"Please, Maria, don't hurt me," Liz pleaded. "I've always tried to be a good friend to you."

"You were as false as all the others. You tolerated me because Dana was my friend. Well, she was, right up until she cheated on me with Patrick."

"What?" Liz turned swiftly, and the knife sliced her throat deeper. "Don't do this. Listen to the inspector. She'll get you the help you need. If killing Dana was a mistake, they can't throw a murder charge at you. Tell her, Inspector, that's right, isn't it?"

"That's right. We can go down the manslaughter route and get you a lesser sentence, Maria. Just put the knife down."

Maria tipped her head back and laughed. "And what if it was intentional? Premeditated, what then? That's murder, isn't it? It doesn't matter what you want to call it, the fact is that I killed that fucking bitch and left her in my gran's house to rot."

"I spoke to Charles in Australia earlier, he was shocked to learn of your involvement and that you used the house to store Dana's body."

"Good. He deserved it. He let me down. Refused to let me rent the place while he was out there. All I wanted was to be close to my gran, she was the only person in this life who truly loved me. Neither my mother nor father did over the years. Always looking for negatives in every step I took throughout my childhood. Gran was my greatest salvation."

Sally frowned, puzzled. "Why didn't she provide for you in her will?"

Maria's gaze dropped, and she scuffed at the leaves beneath her feet. She didn't respond, so Sally repeated the question.

"I want to understand… Why didn't she provide for you in her will?"

Maria's gaze sought out Sally's, and her eyes narrowed. "Because I stole from her. That was her punishment for me. When she was alive, she forgave me, or said she had, but the opposite was true. In the end, she turned out to be the same as every other fucker in my life. They've all treated me like a second-class citizen."

"We didn't," Liz dared to retaliate. "I was your friend."

"Were you, Liz? Where were you when those two boys jumped me in the playground at school and beat the shit out of me for spoiling their game of football?"

"That was years ago, Maria."

"Yeah, well, I'm like a frigging elephant, I never forget, and why should I? I stuck around with you guys long enough to hatch a plan to punish you all. The inspector here, discovering Dana's body, forced my hand."

"Are you telling me all Dana's friends and family have wronged you in the past, Maria? All of them?"

"Every last one of them. Deep down, I know they blamed me for what happened to Dana when she went missing."

"You're insane. We were right, if you're the one who killed her. How warped are you?" Liz had the courage to say. She twisted to challenge Maria, and the knife sliced her throat deeper. "Go on, fucking kill me. I'm depressed, I can't wait for the end to come. Get on with it, or has your bottle gone these days? All these attacks on Dana's loved ones have amounted to nothing. That must have come as a bitter blow to you, right?"

"Maybe it was intentional," Maria snarled.

"And maybe you're not as brave as you think you are," Liz challenged her.

Sally spotted Lorne break cover behind the two women, and Sally prepared to make her move. She nodded, and they both crept forward. Sally grabbed Maria's wrist, and the movement caught her off-guard, and she dropped the knife.

Lorne swooped and whisked Liz from Maria's grasp and marched her out of harm's way. Maria realised her options were limited and fell to the ground to search for the knife, but Sally saw the tip of the blade glint in the sunlight and kicked it away.

Maria growled, bared her teeth, lowered her head and charged at Sally. Sally had the sense to take a step to the side before Maria made contact with her stomach. Maria grunted as she fell facedown in a pile of leaves. The rest of the team emerged from their shelter behind several trees in the area and pounced on Maria. Within seconds, she was cuffed and taken away, shouting expletives to anyone enjoying the peace and quiet of their surroundings who cared to listen.

"Are you okay?" Lorne asked Sally.

"I am. How are you, Liz? You were brave, sticking up to her like that when she had a knife against your throat." Sally checked the wound over and wiped the excess blood away on a tissue. "It's superficial, no lasting damage done."

"What do I have to live for? I have nothing, therefore, it made sense for me to take the risk. It worked, too. It gave you the opportunity to tackle her."

Sally patted Liz on the shoulder. "You were still extremely brave. We're grateful for you literally putting your neck on the line for us. Next time, leave it for us to sort out, you hear me?" she chastised with a grin.

Liz smiled. "I'd do it all over again if it meant all of us getting out of the situation alive. She's one twisted fucker. It's bullshit what she said about the gang, of course. I don't know if what she said is true about her fella and Dana having a fling, though. I can't see it somehow. Maria is the one with the twisted mind, Dana wasn't, and yet she was the one who paid the price for probably having it out with her that night."

"We'll interview her when we get back to the station. Hopefully we'll find out what really happened, that is, if she doesn't go down the 'no comment' route. We'll see. Come on, let's get you home, although I'd rather you go to the hospital to get checked over, but I don't think you're going to entertain that, are you?"

Liz smiled. "Don't worry about me. I need you to concentrate on getting all you can out of that bitch. What about the family? They should be told."

"You're right, I'll ring them once we get you back to the car."

THE INTERVIEW TOOK place a few hours later, once a duty solicitor had arrived. Lorne said the necessary verbiage to commence the interview.

Then it was down to Sally to ask her first question. "Why did you kill Dana Caldwell, Maria?"

Maria stared at her, ground her teeth and let out a deranged laugh.

Sally repeated the same question over and over until finally, Maria said, "She deserved to die. Every cheating bastard on this planet deserves to die for what they put their friends through."

"We only have your word that she was cheating. Her husband wasn't aware of any affair she may have had with your boyfriend at the time."

"He would say that. He didn't care. He was away from home most weeks, shagging all and sundry, no doubt, in his absence."

"You truly believe that?"

"Yes, don't you?"

"No. Some people in this life do what's necessary to earn a decent living and provide for their loved ones."

She lifted her head and smirked at Sally. "You reckon? You're as deluded as they are. Dana swooped. As soon as

Patrick gave her the eye, she was in there. It didn't matter that we, as friends, had years behind us. All that went out the window as soon as she parted her legs for him, the bitch. She denied it, of course."

"Why would she deny it at a time when her life is in danger?"

Maria appeared to drift off, and the truth tumbled out of her mouth. Sally sat back and let Maria tell all with no interruptions.

"I beat the crap out of her that night. Broke her nose. Left her lying on the path while I ran home to fetch the car. I picked up the keys to the house and returned to where I left Dana. She was still out cold. I summoned up the strength to get her in the car and pulled her out of it at the other end. I kept her at the house, tied up for days. I wanted to make her suffer and stopped feeding her after a couple of days. I ordered her upstairs to the bedroom. She started a fight. I hit her with a metal bar and heard her bones snap. She pushed me to my limits and suffered the consequences."

"So you left her there to die, is that it?"

"Yes. I went back after a week or so, untied her hands and feet and left her there to rot. I knew if she was ever found that it would confuse people, her not being bound by restraints." She grinned at Sally. "I did good, didn't I?"

You warped frigging arsehole! Sally tutted and shook her head. "Evidently not, otherwise you wouldn't be sitting here being interviewed about Dana's murder. Correction, I've heard enough, make that being *charged* with Dana's murder. Sergeant Warner, get the custody sergeant in here to do the necessary."

Lorne left her seat. Even the duty solicitor didn't bother fighting Maria's corner. She was taken down to the custody suite to be formally charged, and Sally and Lorne trudged up the stairs on weary legs.

"I could do with a gallon of coffee. Feel I've missed out during the day. Is it just me, or does everyone feel drained once a suspect has been caught?" Sally asked.

"I used to feel the same, sometimes," Lorne admitted.

"Ah, here she is now. Hold on, Donna." Joanna raised her hand and held the phone out to Sally.

Her steps were hesitant. Was it bad news? Was Donna about to tell her that Jack had gone? She perched on the desk and closed her eyes. "Donna. Is everything all right?"

"Hey, you sound tired."

"No more than usual, hon. Dare I ask how Jack is?"

"I thought you'd want to be the first to know."

Oh God, no!

"Know what? Please, don't keep me in suspense any longer than is necessary, Donna."

"He's going to make it. He's come round. He wants to see you."

Sally broke down, and Lorne was the first to comfort her.

"What's wrong, Sal? Come on, tell me."

"Hello, Sally. Are you still there?"

Lorne prised the phone from Sally's clenched hand. "Donna, it's Lorne. What's going on?"

"Is Sally all right?"

"Sort of."

"It's Jack, he's awake, he's going to be fine, eventually. He wants to see her."

"Bloody hell. That's fabulous news. You must be thrilled."

"I haven't quite figured out how I feel yet. Can I tell him to expect Sally soon?"

"We're on our way. I'll drive her there myself."

EPILOGUE

*L*orne drove to the hospital. Sally was lost deep in thought during the journey. They held hands as they ran through the corridors to ICU. Donna was there, waiting for them in the corridor.

They shared a group hug, and Donna wiped the tears away from Sally's eyes.

"Hey, he won't want to see you like this," Donna warned, clearly the strongest of them all now.

"I know. It's a mixture of relief and happiness, so they're definitely good tears."

"He's amazed the staff with his recovery."

"Did they bring him out of the coma?" Sally asked, confused.

"They kept a close eye on his statistics and decided it was for the best. Anyway, enough about that, he's eager to see you, both of you."

They pulled on a protective apron and a mask and applied sanitiser at the door then walked onto the ward.

The nurse on duty smiled and nodded at them then

placed a finger on her lips. "Please be quiet and respectful to the other patients."

Sally and Lorne gave her the thumbs-up and followed Donna down the ward to Jack's bed. She drew back the curtain. Jack was propped up against a couple of pillows, his skin sallower than usual, but he was alive. A smile touched his partially cracked lips, and he raised a weak hand for Sally to take.

She couldn't help it, the tears refused to remain subdued. She slipped her hand in his and bent down to kiss him on the cheek. "Hello, you. I see you're still hanging around in all the best places."

He smiled. "And I'm still doing things that will attract an audience. How's the investigation going?"

Sally sat in the chair next to him while Donna and Lorne held back, near the foot of the bed. "You really want to do this?"

"Yes. Don't tell me you've caught the bastard?"

"Of course. Even in your absence we're a shit-hot team."

"Well, who is it?"

"Guess."

Jack rolled his eyes and rested his head against the pillow. "I'm too tired to play games. Just tell me, Sally."

"I apologise. It was Maria Adams."

His head lifted a touch, and he stared at her. "Of all the people… I never saw that one coming. I knew I was losing my touch."

"Nonsense. She had us all fooled. She's played the family for years, they were as shocked as we were. Sod the investigation, tell me how you're feeling, and don't say like a lorry hit you."

"Why not? It's the damn truth. I didn't think I was going to make it for a while back there, but the doctors have said I've made a miraculous recovery, and that's down to Donna being by my side day and night." He held out a hand, and Donna slid hers into it.

"Where else would I be?" Donna asked.

Tears bulged in his eyes, and his gaze sought out Lorne's. "Hey, come closer, Lorne. I've got something I want to say to you."

Lorne shuffled alongside the bed and clutched his other hand. "It's good to see you, Jack, you had us all worried there for a day or two."

"Thanks for stepping in for me. I hope you didn't take any bullshit from the boss in my absence."

"No, she was as good as gold. Putty in my hand. You've trained her well, Jack."

Sally raised an eyebrow. "Do you two mind? I am here, you know."

"I'm grateful you're both here. Donna and I have been talking, and we've decided it's time."

"For what?" Sally dared to ask. She feared what his answer was going to be.

"Time for me to hang up my handcuffs for the final time."

"You can't do that, Jack, what will I do without you to have a go at every day?" Sally jested, fighting back the emotions ripping through her.

"I've made my decision, Sal, we both have. Donna and I have been discussing what to do with our lives going forward, and remaining with the force isn't an option. Hey, they're likely to kick me out anyway, what with the injuries I've sustained. I'm even more useless now than when they discharged me from the army. I'm tired of living in the fast lane. It's time to take my foot off the pedal and enjoy the rest of my life, without feeling anxious all the time."

"If that's what you want, Jack, neither I nor anyone else is going to stand in your way." Sally's voice caught in her throat.

"Not like that was an option," he replied. "Anyway, I'm leaving you in the safest hands possible. There was a reason Lorne decided to join us, and this is it."

"No, that's not true, Jack," Lorne stated, obviously as choked as Sally.

"It might not be true, but it's how it's going to end up." He reached for Sally's hand again and squeezed it tightly. "Onwards and upwards for both of us, boss. This is the end of a beautiful partnership."

Sally swallowed down the lump lodged in her throat. "But not the end of our friendship, I hope."

Jack smiled, laughed then winced in pain. "You can't get rid of me that easily."

"Here's to yours and Donna's future. May it be long and healthy from this day forward."

They all raised an imaginary glass of bubbly and chinked it together. "To Jack and Donna."

THE END

Thank you for reading Where Did She Go? The next book in this cold case series **Sinner** is now available.

In the meantime, have you read any of my fast paced other crime thrillers yet? Why not try the first book in the DI Sara Ramsey series No Right to Kill

Or grab the first book in the bestselling, award-winning, Justice series here, Cruel Justice.

. . .

OR THE FIRST book in the spin-off Justice Again series, Gone In Seconds.

WHY NOT TRY the first book in the DI Sam Cobbs series, set in the beautiful Lake District, To Die For.

PERHAPS YOU'D PREFER to try one of my other police procedural series, the DI Kayli Bright series which begins with The Missing Children.

OR MAYBE YOU'D enjoy the DI Sally Parker series set in Norfolk, Wrong Place.

OR MY GRITTY police procedural starring DI Nelson set in Manchester, Torn Apart.

OR MAYBE YOU'D like to try one of my successful psychological thrillers She's Gone, I KNOW THE TRUTH or Shattered Lives.

KEEP IN TOUCH WITH M A COMLEY

Pick up a FREE novella by signing up to my newsletter today.
https://BookHip.com/WBRTGW

BookBub
www.bookbub.com/authors/m-a-comley

Blog

http://melcomley.blogspot.com

Why not join my special Facebook group to take part in monthly giveaways.

Readers' Group

Printed in Great Britain
by Amazon